THE

WALKING

SON

PRAISE FOR THE WALKING SON

"The Walking Son by Eddie Generous evokes Stephen King's Thinner as a dead man's curse sends a desperate couple on a terrifying road trip deep into the heart of the haunted American South. Dark and unsettling...a page-turner all the way through to its bitter, if hopeful, end."
- Blu Gilliand, Cemetery Dance

'The Walking Son is an enthralling, intriguing blend of mystery, suspense, a deadly curse, and ghostly witchery. I defy you to put it down before you have devoured every last delicious morsel."

- Catherine Cavendish, author of 'In Darkness, Shadows Breathe'

ALSO BY EDDIE GENEROUS

NOVELLAS

Behemoth Risen
What Lurks Beneath
The Breach
Savage Beasts of the Arctic Circle
Plantation Pan
Rawr
Trouble at Camp Still Waters
Great Big Teeth

NOVELS

Hetty (forthcoming)
Burn Scars
Camp Summit
Radio Run

COLLECTIONS

Dusk
Tales from the Meat Wagon
Dead Is Dead But Not Always

THE WALKING SON

EDDIE GENEROUS

Cover and Titles by
Konn Lavery

THE SEVENTH TERRACE

Ruthie's was the only place open at midnight for two hundred miles, and it was about to close. Sonya Wright had a bill in her left hand and pot of thrice-reheated coffee in her right. "You staying somewhere? I saw you hop out of Darnel's pickup."

The thin man with a scruffy beard and close-set eyes, clothes damp and dirty, boots sopping, simply grinned from where he sat on the faded red vinyl seat. He made his fingers walk on air.

"You ain't gonna get anywhere tonight," Sonya said, slipping the bill onto the table. The man had drunk three large cups of coffee in about half an hour. Sonya had served him a to-go cup on account of how he looked, and how he smelled, and her general opinion of hitchhikers, but she was warming to the fact he hadn't caused any trouble.

The man licked his lips. They were pasty, gooey with saliva. "I'm always somewhere, even when nobody sees me," he said through a thick American South accent. "My mother had called it my magic trick, though it was she who dabbled in magics."

"You from way down, huh?" Sonya said and filled the man's cup without waiting for his answer. She'd go turn the sign to closed just as soon as she did her polite diligence.

The man nodded and lifted his cup in thanks.

"Where you from?" she asked.

"Alabama. My family, we were never travelers, but I changed that. That said, no matter how far I go or where I end up, I never truly leave home." He touched his chest.

Sonya squinted her right eye, then nodded backward with a grin. "Hey, yeah, like you always got home in you. Like the accent. All I know about down there are the movies and TV stuff. Scary—ooh and that bridge: Selma."

"Selma, yes. I know Selma. Should know Selma, it's not far from my home."

"Cool. So, what're you doing in British Columbia?"

The man made his fingers walk again. Sonya's eyes followed them, narrowing in on the dirt beneath his nails. The sight broke a spell and she hurried to the door to flip the sign, got busy clearing the two plates left at tables, and then headed on to the back. She suspected in a fair fight, she could probably wipe the floor with the man, but men didn't always fight fair and she was alone. Best to wait for him to leave.

It was only minutes after draining the sink that she heard the jingle of the bell hung on the inside of the door. She followed the sound out and discovered the man had paid in change. He'd left three American half-dollar coins and two dimes. The year bevelled onto all three was 1876.

"Geez Louise," Sonya said, thinking she'd swap out new change for the till and test the value of those coins on eBay. "What a weirdo."

"You did what?" Stephen Barber said into his cellphone after draping a stained and musty pocket paperback of Donald Westlake's *The Busy Body* over his knee.

It was after two in the morning. The closer it came to the date the tenants were to move in, the less his mind ever seemed to settle. He had invested every dollar he'd ever saved, borrowed to his limits, and had sold off an inherited—and cherished—book collection.

"Man, this guy...he came outta nowhere," Riley Hautala said. "We were coming back from the lodge and...shit."

Riley and a woman named Rosemary Young were Stephen's investment partners in the apartment complex. Riley and Rosemary were both better off than Stephen, but not by much. Riley was an insurance agent and had sold several properties to come up with the capital investment. He had kept his small hunting cabin—unbeknownst to his wife—as the value wasn't great and selling it meant he'd have nowhere to take his *mistress*/business partner.

Rosemary was chief of the Shiny River police department, and of old money. Her settling up an equal share of the investment was a little easier, but she'd still had to sell off four vintage Ford Mustangs, leaving her with only her police cruiser and an aged, but fine,

1999 Ford Ranger. She also had the family home to borrow against—a sprawling property with three cottages aside from the main house, a natural hot spring, and a seasonal rental income. Her husband had died six years earlier, shortly after she'd hit thirty-one, and she hadn't remarried, probably because the man she was seeing was still married to Mrs. Riley Hautala.

"So what?" Stephen said.

"He's dead and Rosemary has an idea...if this comes out, it's all our asses," Riley said.

Stephen hurried out of his bedroom—his wife had almost certainly awakened by the sound of his answering the call. "What do you mean, it's all our asses?"

"If it gets out, we're cooked."

"What?"

"Rosemary was driving and, man...it can't get out. It wasn't her fault, but...man, just bring your mixer and a couple bags of cement."

"You better be playing." Stephen ran his hand over the spiky fuzz rising from his scalp. He'd shaved it down a few weeks earlier, but it was starting to look like hair again.

"Man, no playing. If this gets out, what do you think happens to the apartments?"

Stephen ground his teeth, seeing everything he'd worked for disappear in a flash because he'd chosen poor business partners. Not that there was much of a choice, really. The people of Shiny River were oil grunts and smelter laborers—which made affordable housing a little less affordable and less available—they weren't investors.

"Just grab your mixer, and whatever else we'll need, and meet up at the site."

"You're a sonofabitch," Stephen said, but not into the phone. He'd already hung up and was heading back to his bedroom to get dressed.

The lump on the bed, Moira, hardly moved, but it did speak. "What're you doing?"

"Have to go out, some water thing at the site."

"Of course."

By the time he was dressed, he'd awoken their son, Paul. He was sixteen, and surprisingly, an all-around respectable and respectful sixteen-year-old.

"You want me to come help?" Paul asked. He was in his boxer shorts and a t-shirt looking downright gangly where he stood in front of the kitchen cupboards, a distant light playing shadows off the stalks of his legs onto the floor.

"Nah, just some bullshit thing. It'll be mostly waiting around."

"Okay." Paul ambled back to his bedroom, munching on a chocolate chip cookie.

The man didn't look dead, not even with blood glistening in his beard, not even with his hips violently askew, not even with his arm twisted behind his back at a cringe-inducing angle. He looked at least a little bit alive in the eyes, perhaps more than a little bit. They seemed to follow the trio as they worked on the open section of flooring around the sump pumps—installed just that afternoon—in the basement of the building's drywall dusty boiler room. The rebar had been laid and the plan was to pour Monday morning when the crews got back to finishing up down there. Most of the recent activity took place in the units—the paint was dry in forty of them and the carpet was down in twenty-one.

But they'd been made to wait for the sump pumps to come in and couldn't finish that patch of flooring until they were installed. Stephen knew this, but Rosemary and Riley didn't, because they didn't work the site, because they didn't have their entire life riding on the success of the venture, and because, simply, they weren't contractors.

When Stephen saw the way they leaned, and smelled the liquor on them, he made them dig deep, as he stood topside, looking at the body.

"Won't be anybody looking for him," Rosemary said and then burped. "Heard on the radio, he's been hitching for more than a month."

"Y'all keep track of that, huh?" Stephen said, feeling sick. "What if he's got family?"

Rosemary ignored the second bit. "Yeah, it's noted these days. Hitchhiking is illegal, but it's usually easier to let a guy move on through than file paperwork, if that's what he's doing."

"Uh huh," Stephen said and knelt, taking the man's wallet from his shirt pocket where Riley had stashed it after taking a peek. There were no cards, nothing from VISA or State Farm or Blockbuster Video. There were no slips of paper aside from a single, very old photograph of a woman—no explanation written on the back. Nothing gave away the man's identity. The only other items in the wallet were three very old American coins. One nickel. One dime. One quarter.

"How deep?" Riley asked. He was a lazy sort when it came to manual labor—aside from pulling a moose or deer out of the bush and hanging it to skin.

Stephen blinked at an image coming to mind: Riley grinning beneath the bust of the dead hitchhiker on the wall, between a moose rack and bear claw. He shook his head and placed the wallet and stack of coins onto the dead man's chest. He then stood, his knees cracking like damp twigs, and stepped to the eight-foot-long gulley where the vented pump covers rose like desert cacti. Riley and Rosemary had dug the loose gravel out all the way to the natural dirt beneath—about four feet.

"Probably that's far enough. This is totally fucked, you know?" Stephen shook his head.

Rosemary's expression was hard as she climbed from the hole. She was a pretty woman, but right then, she looked too much like her father—the meanest cop the county had ever endured. She brushed off her hands and bent to grab the man's wallet and the coins. The wallet went into the hole and the coins went into her pocket.

"Come on out, then," she said to Riley, taking hold of the dead man's feet.

Stephen hadn't touched the man aside from pulling out the wallet and wasn't about to. He made for the cement mixer and the garden hose with the spray attachment. The cement was already soft, but he fed it another healthy spray before he got back to turning the crank.

Riley grabbed the dead man and lifted him by the armpits. "He sure stinks."

Rosemary simply grunted and said, "On three. One, two, three," and they tossed the corpse into the gulley.

Stephen tried not to look, but couldn't help it. "Okay, Riley, shovel in some of what you dug. Rosemary, get ready to shovel gravel into my mix."

Riley was slow enough that Stephen snatched the shovel and got busy. "Cool it, man," Riley said, but Stephen did not. He was tired, scared, and starting to feel guilty. He tossed the shovel and returned to the mixer handle after looking in on the mix.

The cement oozed into the gulley and Rosemary lifted a shovelful in askance. Stephen nodded to the gulley and she started a slow scoop. Stephen grabbed more cement and got to mixing another batch, telling Rosemary to switch targets with her shovel. The gravel went into the mixer and then the cement went onto the already disappeared corpse.

As Stephen worked a hand trowel from his knees, the others loomed. Paranoid, he stole glances over his shoulder—what if they meant to kill him, too?

"We should've just did it out by the dumpster or something," Riley said.

Stephen shook his head. "No, we shouldn't. One of the foremen would've asked me why. They might even ask who poured this concrete when it was going to pour Monday anyway, but maybe not."

"The man with all the answers," Riley said, condescending.

Of the trio, Stephen was the only one without a college diploma and sometimes he felt it in the way Riley and Rosemary spoke to him. This despite that he'd quarterbacked the deal between them and that he'd drawn the blueprints from scratch.

"You know, I can finish up on my own," Stephen said.

Riley turned to leave, but Rosemary spoke before he took a step toward the stairs. "We have one more point to discuss."

Stephen's heart pattered like a hummingbird and the hand holding the trowel slowed. They were going to kill him and bury him next to the nameless hitchhiker.

He said, "Oh, and what's that?"

"It's like I'm collecting funny money," Sonya said, picking up the brown two-dollar bill—pulled from circulation in 1996—left behind as a tip by a departing Mennonite couple.

Stephen thought nothing of it from where he sat, drinking his first coffee of the day, despite it being almost two in the afternoon. He'd slept in and had to get away from his family as soon as he rose. They made him feel doubly guilty, though not as much as the old coin in his pocket.

"Here," Rosemary had said, flipping Stephen and Riley each a coin from the dead man's wallet. "Keep that as a reminder, we're all in this together."

Riley had scoffed then. "I only got the nickel." As if it was about dollar value and not about all three of them holding the guillotine's rope while the blade hung over their necks.

Stephen had the quarter, leaving Rosemary with the dime.

"What do you mean?" the daytime and evening cook, Chubb Hughes, asked through the order window.

"Last night, some dirty guy with a big long beard paid in coins from eighteen-seventy-something. I checked eBay, probably going to come away with a fifty-buck tip at the end of it."

"Smooth," Chubb said.

Stephen could almost feel that coin in his pocket heating up. He turned slightly in his seat so that his right ear had a better angle on the conversation.

Sonya took a twoonie from her black apron and swapped it for the brown bill. It was crisp enough to give her high hopes. "Look at that, more than a hundred years newer than last night's money," she said after reading the date stamped on the bill.

"You'd think a guy would know about old coins being worth more. If he has them, I mean," Chubb said.

"I don't know. He was a hitchhiker, had a long beard, real skinny. Said he was from Alabama. Pretty weird. When I asked him where he was going, he did one of these," Sonya said and made the finger walking gesture.

"Ha, he a real-life Forrest Gump?"

Sonya laughed. "Hey, yeah, maybe. I didn't even think of that. You see Tom Hanks doing Mr. Rogers?"

With the conversation shifted, Stephen turned his attention back to his coffee. There was no doubt it was the same man and that meant people had seen him around, meaning people might wonder where he went. He slammed back the coffee and stood quickly enough to send his chair legs screeching along the floor. "Sorry," he said and dug into his pocket. He pulled out the quarter with the rest of his change, and for a moment, considered handing it off, but couldn't do it.

"What are you doing out here?" Rosemary said after parking on the far side shoulder and leaning over the pitted cement railing of the old stone bridge on Whitmore Road.

Stephen jerked around, pulled from thoughtless reverie. He hadn't heard her coming, in fact, had reached as close to calm as he'd been since awaking seven hours earlier. The sun was still plenty high, but the breeze carried a subtle chill.

"I'm just sitting here. What, there a law against that?" Stephen said.

"No, no law." Rosemary's voice was calm.

"So, what's the problem?"

"Problem is, a man ought to look as normal as he can after committing a crime; he draws attention otherwise. Problem is, I've never seen you sitting out here, not ever, and now here you are. That's acting out of character."

"I can't look at them," Stephen said quickly. "What if the dead guy has a family out there wondering where he is?"

"They'd be wondering anyway. Now, I'm more worried about your family, wondering where you are. How come dear old dad is acting so funny?"

"When I loo–"

"Get your shit together, Barber!" Rosemary barked this single order with enough authority in her voice that Stephen almost fell off the bridge. "Go home, pretend everything is normal until it is normal. It's like sleeping, fake it until suddenly you're doing it."

Stephen turned and kicked his legs over the edge and pushed to standing. "I never asked for this and you put it on me. What kind of police chief drives drunk?" Stephen said, finger stabbed out with piles of silent accusation.

Rosemary snorted. "All of us. Every damned one of us. Now go the fuck home, Barber."

Stephen did, and when he got there, he did his best to play like everything was normal and right and he hadn't buried a stranger beneath several feet of gravel and cement.

The more he hung around, the easier it got. He and Paul watched a feature about the '93 Canadiens Stanley Cup run, and later, he and Moira took a walk along the river that cut the town down the middle. By a quarter to seven, Stephen thought he might be able to forget about the whole mess, enough to go about life anyway. He settled into his recliner with the Westlake paperback—taking a moment to again mourn the sacrificial loss of a fine first edition of *The Mercenaries*–when a text from Riley pinged his message box, asking if he wanted to visit for a beer.

Unfortunately, Moira had snuck in and was standing over his shoulder as he read the message and she encouraged him to go. For the sake of normalcy, he did the Saturday ritual, and went to drink beer with a friend.

"You don't think that nasty bastard got me sick, do ya?" Riley had led Stephen into the den. Lined together like a weak anthropological exhibit on types of Canadian Cervidae were three sets of racks: elk, moose, and mule deer. A line of hooks featured close to a dozen overlapping baseball caps from companies like Rapala, Browning, and Sitka. Centering the space was a TV big enough that it made the home seem secondary, as if it had come first and everything else molded around it to give it shelter. On the screen was *Ironman 3* in vivid HD. Riley handed over a Coors Light, and once they sat, began pressing the two strange bumps that had formed on his forehead. "You think he had some kind of man-eating ticks on him and they got into me?"

Stephen scrunched up his face and leaned in close to inspect the bumps. "If he did, you deserve it," he said and then added, "We all do."

Riley flipped his wrist at this. "Bull. He was pret'near standing in the middle of the damned road."

"Or did it look like that because you had a date with Captain Morgan?"

Riley put his hand to his chest. "I am appalled that you'd suggest I'd drink anything less than Appleton Estates." The humored visage fell, and he recommenced prodding at the bumps—nubs, really. "I got something going on."

"Yeah."

After a few minutes of silence, aside from the crash-bang of *Ironman 3*, Riley leaned close and said, "Rosemary said you were sitting at the bridge. You're not gonna fuck us on this, right?"

Stephen clicked his tongue, and without turning to face his friend, said, "Way I see it, you two kind of fucked *me* on this. I was at home, in bed, sober. You two were out, what, fucking in your shack? Getting drunk, maybe a little stoned?"

"Quiet," Riley said and looked over his shoulder to the staircase. "Rosemary's just a little worried, that's all."

Stephen took the full beer by the neck and drained it in about six seconds. "Ahh, thanks for the brew, *bud*." He stepped around Riley and headed for the back door.

"You don't want to test Rosemary, man," he said.

Stephen didn't slow until reaching the door. He opened it and left without giving Riley even a glance at his face. It felt like a minor victory, problem was, he couldn't go home yet, because like it or not, Rosemary was right and he needed to keep up appearances.

He drove to Willie's Liquor Barn and picked up a six-pack of Heineken. He headed for the site—construction and burial—and parked around back. He pulled his cellphone from his pocket and continued *The Murder List* on audiobook where he'd left off, popping caps with a jackknife, and watching the night through his windshield.

The most exciting point of it all was when he had to scratch matching itches on both feet simultaneously. Once the beer bottles were empty, he drove home, placed his wallet and stack of change on the dresser, and joined his wife beneath the covers.

If nothing else, with seven beers in him, he was apt to fall asleep before the sun came up.

Sunday was a quiet day at home and Stephen settled to putter in a purely natural manner, and just like Rosemary suggested, and just like sleeping, the act of imitating normal became natural. By the end of the day, he was tired and fully willing to veg out on the couch to watch Netflix with Moira and Paul. In fact, he was feeling almost good until Monday morning rolled around and he grabbed his wallet and the stack of coins.

The 1876 American quarter was gone.

In its place were two dimes and three pennies, all American, all from 1876.

His breath hitched as he looked at the heavy money—so easily separated from modern coins. There was no questioning the difference, but there was also no questioning where the 1876 money came from...unless he'd accidentally spent the quarter and got change.

But no. The penny was out of circulation and without value in Canada. Nobody would've given him change in pennies, if they had, he would've called them out on it. And the year...*how is* that *possible?*

The old coins went into his left pocket and the rest went into his right, with the wallet. He stepped through his quiet home on unsteady legs with his cellphone and lunch pail in his hands. He had to tell himself to breathe easy, had to tell himself to keep calm.

He opened the truck door and slipped inside. It still smelled a little like beer. He closed the door and shouted, "What in the ever-loving Christ is going on!" He dropped the lunch pail onto the passenger's seat and fiddled with his phone. He found Riley's cell number and dialed it.

Being as it wasn't even six-thirty yet, the call went straight to voicemail. Stephen hit END and started the truck. The index finger of his right hand tapped on the dash and he chewed at dried skin on his lip while he gazed vacantly at his home. He might've stayed there all day if Moira hadn't stepped to the bay window to frown down at him. He gave a quick salute and backed out the lane.

Acting without thought, he drove to Ruthie's for a coffee. That early, Ruthie's was a boy's club of farmers and contractors. They'd sit and talk shop, talk world news, and complain a blue streak about politics and taxes. The last thing Stephen wanted was conversation, but his mind was too busy and his body was going through the everyday motions.

Ruthie Jean was about eighty and had worked six days a week—aside from three weeks off around Christmas—for as long as Stephen could remember, which included days when his father had dragged him out of bed early to go out for breakfast before getting to the chores. Thirty, forty, fifty years? He'd never ask and wasn't too concerned about it right then as she filled the porcelain mug by the seat he'd taken at the big communal table.

"Just coffee?" she asked and Stephen nodded.

Down the table, an old four-foot-tall polio surviving great grandfather named Elmer said, in his high voice, "How goes the apartments?"

Stephen blinked at him. "Just poured in the floor around the sump pumps."

"Oh, I thought you were darn near done."

A few of the other men looked at Stephen. The apartments were big news in a town where workers often slept in tents or stacked up like sardines in granny suites in locals' basements, especially since the camps were getting harder and harder to keep sanitary with all the viruses floating around recently.

"We are. It is. First of August, still running on schedule," Stephen said, finding the words coming a little more easily. He didn't add that was often because he, Moira, and Paul spent many nights picking up where the guys left off at five o'clock. "A handful would be ready by the end of the week, but there's too much going on to move in."

"What kind of appliances you running in there?" another man said.

Stephen squinted, thinking. "Uh, Danby. I actually talked to the president of the company when I put the order through."

An old farmer with huge dentures pointed an empty fork at Stephen. "He's a good one. Helped a bunch of Syrians to come over and get started."

At a solo table in the corner, another farmer grunted. "Like we need'm here."

The old farmer turned on his seat and started to lay into the other man. Breakfast played out fairly normally from there and Stephen felt his body relaxing, until it came time to pay and he stood, felt and heard the jingling within his left side pocket.

First thing he did, once back to his truck, was dial Riley again. The man didn't answer his cellphone, so Stephen dialed his landline. Riley's wife, Susan, answered and said her poor hubby must've drank too many adult sody pops on the weekend because he wasn't getting out of bed.

Perhaps the slowest day in the history of slow days, Stephen checked the clock on his cellphone every half hour and texted Riley a dozen times without response. He ate his lunch in the boiler room basement, looking at all that clean cement, and used the coolness of the space as an excuse when one of the guys laying carpet asked him why he was down there *all by hisself.*

By the time Stephen had burned up the hour, six other guys were down there with him. One young laborer sat with his back against the wall and his feet directly above the resting place of the anonymous hitchhiker.

Twice Stephen had light hallucinations about gnarled hands bursting free through a dust cloud and taking hold of the young man.

For the first time since construction began, Stephen Barber was the first man off the lot at five o'clock. He'd called Riley's cellphone and got no answer, decided rather than talking to the Susan again that he'd just make an appearance. It wasn't far–nothing in town was far–but when he got there, nobody was home. Riley's truck was in the driveway, but his wife's Cadillac was gone.

"Where are you, you sonofabitch?" Stephen said. He reached into his left front pocket and withdrew the old coins. Nothing had changed.

"What's wrong with your feet?" Moira said.

They were on the couch after supper. Moira was watching *The Outsider* and Stephen was reading a back issue of Alfred Hitchcock's

Mystery Magazine while rubbing his bare feet on the rug to scratch away the dual itchiness.

"Might have athlete's foot or something," he said.

Moira bunched up her facial features. "Better not give it to me."

"What's mine is yours, dear," Stephen said, absently.

"I'll remember that."

It was Stephen's turn to make a face.

At Ruthie's the next morning, Stephen had his phone out and was sending yet another text message to Riley when the hospital's janitor broke a bit of gossip.

"That Riley Hautala's in rough shape."

Stephen blinked and jerked his head up. The skinny janitor, all teeth and bulging eyes, was leering at Stephen.

"What?"

"He's got flesh-eating disease or something like it. They had to rush him to Vancouver. Whole body's covered in the stuff. Got him looking like a mummy."

"Holy, it ain't catching is it?" Elmer asked. Catching polio as a boy made him paranoid about catching everything else. "We won't be quarantined again, right?"

"Nah, but they don't know how he contracted it or if it's even what they suspect. Could be anything. Maybe something brand new." The janitor was laying it on, adding all the spookiness of a campfire ghost story. "You see him lately?" he added, asking Stephen.

"Yeah, on Saturday night I went over for a beer."

"What'd he look like?" one of the farmers asked.

"He looked fine," Stephen said, but thought, *aside from those nubs he'd grown.*

Though he didn't care to do it, Stephen stopped by the police station and Rosemary welcomed him into a neat and polished office. "I take it you heard about Riley."

"Yeah. You see him?"

Rosemary shook her head as she reached into her pocket. She pulled out a nickel and a penny. "I've tried to throw them away, but guess what?" Her eyebrows rose. "I've tried to spend it, but guess what?" A sneer formed on her mouth. "I've tried to drop them in the river, but guess what?"

Stephen felt the weight of his own collection of coins—a penny had gone missing that morning. "You tell me, eh."

"How about I show you," she said and started unbuttoning her uniform shirt with quick and nimble fingers. She pulled it wide, revealing a sturdy-looking black bra, a slight roll pillowing over her utility belt, and a strangely shiny silver patch over her chest. Her fingers ran over it and then down to her hip. "Got this here, too. According to Doc Grantham, it isn't the same as what Riley has, though he's equally perplexed. It gets a little bit worse every morning." She tapped the spot on her hip, making a hollow thud, like knocking knuckles against a tetherball pole.

Stephen closed his eyes, that sound, those spots, none of it seemed real, and a string of hope dangled before him. "So you *have* seen him?"

Again, Rosemary shook her head.

"So maybe you're getting it wrong."

Rosemary's nostrils flared. "How about you, you have anything happening?

Stephen's feet ached for a scratch tenfold at her question, but he denied them. "Nothing."

"Lucky. Doc Grantham said Riley has turned brown and the little peach fuzz he had—same as I have and you have and everybody else has—was growing out and stiffening. And bone protuberances sprouted from his forehead. That's what he called them, *protuberances*. He tells me things because I can act like it's a matter of public safety."

"Okay. So, what did he say you have?" Stephen pointed at her chest.

Rosemary smiled and leaned back on her chair as she began mating the buttons with the slits of her shirt. "He doesn't know, but I do."

"What?"

"You believe in God, Barber?"

Stephen jerked away at this like it tasted foul. "No. No."

"I do. I also believe in ghosts and miracles, and curses."

"Fuck off."

"Not a chance. I'm going to see the priest this afternoon, have him bless me, get some holy water. You'd be wise to do the same—oh wait, nothing's bothering you, is it?"

Stephen stood up and the simple act actually helped to quell the intense itchiness. "That's right."

"Of course it is," Rosemary stood and opened her belt and pants, revealing equally practical black underwear and began stuffing her shirt tails inside. "I have a feeling we'll be digging that man up. We did something stupid and we'll pay until we make it right."

This sounded gruesome and awful, but Stephen found the idea of getting right by the dead man made him feel a little easier, too.

The cellphone vibrated on the kitchen counter next to a box of Jos Louis cakes. Stephen checked the name and relief washed over him: Riley.

"Hey, where–?" Stephen's words caught in his mouth when he heard feminine sniffles.

"Stephen, this is Susan Hautala."

Stephen cleared his throat gently. "Hello."

"Riley's dead. He's passed on and he's dead."

"I'm…I'm so sorry. Is there anything…?"

"The visitation's on Friday. Funeral's on Saturday. I need you to be a pallbearer, he would've…would've wanted that."

Stephen closed his eyes and leaned against the counter, his legs going to pudding. "Anything." He paused, searched for the right way to ask. "Susan, how was he sick?"

She burst into tears and through sobbing breaths said, "I can't," and hung up.

Moira stood a foot inside the kitchen, her heels still touching the living room carpet. She had an empty ice cream bowl in her left hand and a spoon in her right. She seemed frozen, as if she'd eaten a bit too much, understanding that something bad had come to pass.

Stephen steadied himself and firmed up his expression. "Riley's dead."

Paul came into the kitchen, sliding on socked feet, and almost nailed his mother as she stepped to Stephen for a hug.

"What?" he said.

Moira ignored him. "That's terrible, was it an accident?"

Stephen almost said yes, but bit it down. "Susan couldn't talk about it."

"Susan who? What happened?" Paul was wide-eyed, almost frantic.

"Riley Hautala is dead," Moira said, her cheek pressed to Stephen's chest.

"No shit."

Stephen nodded somberly to his son.

On the morning of the visitation, Stephen awoke knowing he'd have another penny fewer. Down to eighteen cents, the itch had moved up his legs. Moira's hand lotion helped, but never for very long.

Up before the others was the norm, but Moira was already in the kitchen, quietly making breakfast–Paul remained in bed. Stephen stepped through the hall to the bathroom and lifted the toilet seat. He bent and scratched a big flake of dead skin from his foot. With a disgusted pinch, he picked up the skin and dropped it over the toilet. First it floated like a snowflake and then rode atop the water like a lily pad. A shiver played up his back.

He fished himself out and began pissing. About mid-way through, he noticed the strange black stains lining his feet. They ran perfectly straight with gaps between, but were not solid.

Squiggles.

He finished pissing and bent down, squinting.

Not squiggles, but words.

He flushed the toilet and dropped the seat. He lifted his foot to the cover and looked closer. The words were so small, but he managed, whispering them aloud as he read, "*Pale, shivering, with rigid features and compressed lips, she looked entirely altered.*" The words continued beneath more dead skin. He peeled it back and the flake clung together in a satisfying, six-inch swatch. He dropped this one in the garbage and leaned in again to read further.

"Stephen?" Moira's voice came from right outside the bathroom door.

She couldn't see it, whatever it meant, not until he fully understood what was happening. He dropped his foot to the floor. "Give me a minute," he said.

"I just came to ask if you were hungry."

"Very," he said and didn't have to fake it.

Once he heard her footfalls carry down the hall, he rushed to the bedroom for socks and underwear.

"Come here," Rosemary said. She was in a pantsuit and a ton of makeup, wearing big sunglasses and a brimmed hat. "Closed casket, but come here."

She grabbed onto Stephen's jacket and began pulling him along. Her footfalls clicked against the stone floor in a way that sounded far too heavy. Stephen let himself be led into the closed area, where in less than an hour, a precession would walk by the casket and say their well wishes and peace to the figure hidden inside the box.

Rosemary lifted the casket lid and turned to Stephen, blocking his view. "Riley's wife said the doctors had never seen anything like it, and it was impossible, despite it happening. They wanted to keep the body for testing, but she wouldn't let them. I asked her if he'd had any change in his pockets when they checked into hospital. Two pennies, but she can't find them, assumed they were lucky or something. You ask me, the money's now disappeared like it never was. I have three pennies left, how about you? You got the quarter, could you spare me some change?" She then knocked fingers against her chest. It sounded like a hollow drum.

"I don't know what—"

Rosemary grabbed Stephen by the back of the head and spun him, forcing him to drink up a close in view of what Riley had become. His skin was gone and he'd come to wear a soft brown pelt with white accents. His jaw had stretched out and his teeth had grown, his gums had gone black. From his forehead, two stubby antlers jutted out like incredible special effects makeup.

Stephen pushed back against the hold, but Rosemary wasn't letting up. He swung blindly over his shoulder and his fist came into contact with her temple, sending her sunglasses to the floor. He backed up tight against Riley's casket and Rosemary sneered at him.

"Don't like what you see?" she said.

Her eyeballs were small red light covers, and the contours of her optical orbits seemed shaped for speed, perfectly aligned to the shape of the light cover, and completely hairless.

"What about this?" she said and unbuttoned the top three buttons of her blouse, revealing a Ford emblem in her blotchy pink skin. "So, what did you get? Maybe yours isn't showing yet?"

"You're crazy," Stephen said, feeling the words on his legs like flea bites.

"I have a theory," Rosemary said as she buttoned up. "Riley turned into a deer because that was his favorite thing. I'm turning into a car because that's my favorite thing. What are you gonna be? A power tool of some sort?" She bent to pick up her glasses.

Stephen thought of the words. His father's book coll–*No!*

It was insanity, a strange anomaly mating with coincidence. Maybe they had caught something from the dead man, *maybe?*

"We're digging him up tonight and burying him behind the old church on Wakefield Line. We're going to say a prayer over the body, consecrate the grave with holy water, and beg for the curse to be lifted. You didn't believe me before, but every myth started somewhere. What we did cursed us and we're going to reverse it."

At the far end of the room, the door opened and the funeral director stepped in. "Excuse me this is a closed–" His words ceased as Rosemary, chief of police, turned around.

Stephen gave his dear–deer–friend a final glance before closing the casket.

"You can't leave me here. I hardly know this woman!" Moira hissed as Stephen slipped his feet into his loafers, just inside the Hautala doorway.

They'd done the long day and to Stephen and Moira's surprise, the bereaved woman had no family come to town and she apparently had no good friends. Susan had clung onto Moira and Moira had allowed it, Stephen by her side the entire time, but now Stephen was getting incessant text messages and said there was a problem at the site. One that, for some damned reason, needed *his* attention.

"I'm sorry, I'll be quick as I can, but it's the water again. Something like that could spoil the whole operation."

She frowned at this. "You act like I don't have things to do, too!"

"Text Paul, make him come to sit with you. I promise, once the issue with the pipes is figured out, it's smooth sailing and regular hours until the tenants move in."

"I don't even know this woman," Moira said again, but more to herself as Stephen had already opened the door and was sidling out.

Rosemary had text messaged him more than a dozen times before he got away, ordering his presence and growing more belligerent with each contact. He stopped at home first for a change of clothes and footwear. He took a peek beneath his sock again and the words seemed clearer, at a starker contrast. *Pale, shivering, with rigid features and compressed lips, she looked an entirely altered being.* He pulled out his phone and typed the words into Google.

"What in the hell?" he said.

The words had come from *Uncle Tom's Cabin* by Harriet Beecher Stowe, first published in 1852. He wiped his lips, thinking about a marbled cover with the leather edges, gold lettering, and the huge mold spot eating through the back like cancer. It was the third most valuable book to go at the auction, but it had been his father's favorite. He'd found the book in a steamer trunk when he was twenty-one and demolishing a property the county had claimed after its owner died and none of the family wanted to pay the due property taxes. Stephen's father hadn't been able to sell the book because explaining where it came from would be impossible. He held onto it, cleaned it, dried it out, and in payment, the book had lit a match to coals of an unknown hobby in the man's heart.

"What the hell?" Stephen said again, shaken, two seconds before another text from Rosemary landed. He had no time for memory lane or mooning over the wonders of the universe.

Six minutes later, he reached the tool trailer and withdrew a wheelbarrow, a cement saw, a jackhammer, a pickaxe, two heavy-duty extension cords, and goggles and masks. Carving the cement would take hours, cleaning the mess they were about to make would take even longer.

Of course, if it worked, they could move on, could do right by the man, and time would be on their side once again.

Rosemary had changed into laboring clothes and was waiting in the boiler room. She had cast away the makeup, hat, and sunglasses, and Stephen swallowed rising panic at the sight of her. Her cheeks had taken on that silver, metallic hue and finish. Her lips look hard as steel. The contours of her brow and cheekbones were too sharp and perfect. Her eyes glowed red in the dim light.

"Quit gawking and let's go," she said.

Stephen blinked it away and his body got busy with work he could do in his sleep—so long as the roar of the blades meeting cement didn't wake him up. He cut foot squares with the saw and Rosemary jackhammered them away. She couldn't keep up, and Stephen pickaxed once he'd cut what needed to be cut.

Better than three hours later, they reached the body, though not quite.

"Still don't think we're cursed?" Rosemary said, her voice had taken on a growl, almost like a gunky engine in need of a tune-up.

The clothes were there, but the man was a skeleton, yellowed and scentless. It was as if he'd been down there for decades rather than days. Stephen kept fighting the good fight in his head, reasoning natural possibilities for how the man came to be in such a state.

Rosemary carried the bundle of clothing and bones while Stephen rolled the wheelbarrow loaded with tools over the temporary plywood ramp atop of the stairs. The tools went out and the body went into the back of Stephen's truck. He draped a tarp over it to keep any of it from blowing away.

Traffic was sparse in town, and once they got to Wakefield Line, it was non-existent. Moonlight fought and lost to the trees canopying the slim gravel lane. After two minutes of cutting through pure dark, the trees opened up and the old church on the knoll let pale light play down like a promise from Heaven. The gravestones were like teeth in a rotten mouth: crooked, leaning, broken, gone.

"Park close, my legs hurt," Rosemary said, most of the bark gone, but the sickly rumble had become prominent.

Stephen did as told, eyes ahead. He was having a hard time looking at her. "I can dig it out, if you want, won't take more than a few minutes to bury something so small."

"Someone, not something."

"Right."

He got out of the truck and Rosemary did the same. She pointed to where he should dig and then she sat on the truck bed's gate next to the bundle of bones. Stephen's back was achy and his hands were stiff, but he moved four feet of soil from a spot just about the size of what they came to bury.

"Probably deep enough, eh?" Stephen stepped back, leaned on the shovel.

Rosemary said nothing.

Stephen lifted his head. She had slumped over in the truck. "Hey? Rosemary? Hey?" he said and then hurried over and put his hand on her shoulder. It was cool and hard. "Rosemary?"

She came to and looked around, the lights of her eyes flaring brighter against the darkness. "Ready?" she said, it came out in a combustion engine rumble.

Stephen tipped the shovel handle against the truck and flipped back the tarp. For a moment he thought the skeleton had disappeared, but it merely hid beneath the dark clothing. He gathered it up and carried it gently to the hole.

"Pour this on it," Rosemary said as she reached into her pocket. Her hand came out stiffly, holding a small plastic bottle.

"Holy water?" Stephen asked as he poured the some onto the body. Rosemary didn't answer and when he looked up, she had slumped again. "Hey. Hey!"

She opened her eyes and licked her lips. "Did you pour it on?"

"Yeah, want me to cover it up?"

"Not yet." She cleared her throat and closed her eyes. "The Lord is my Shepherd, I shall not want. He makes me to lie down in green pastures. He leads me beside the still waters. He restores my soul. He leads me on the paths of righteousness for His name's sake. Though I walk through the valley of the shadow of death, I will fear no evil; for Thou art with me. Thy rod and Thy staff, they comfort me. Thou prepare a table before me in the presence of my enemies. Thou anoint my head with oil and my cup runneth over. Surely goodness and mercy shall follow me all the days of my life, and I will dwell in the house of the Lord forever. Amen." The words came out robotically, without any emotion at all.

"Amen," Stephen parroted. "Now cover it?"

"No. Toss in your coins." Stephen blinked, but reached into his pocket.

Rosemary leaned onto the heels of her feet, took three steps, and dropped her coins into the hole before stumbling back.

"Now cover it?" Stephen said.

"Yeah."

Back at the worksite, Rosemary kicked open the door of the truck. "You know, I think I feel a little better already."

Stephen could believe it, because he felt better. Much better. "Good, so you think it worked?"

"Better have." She closed the door behind her and walked stiffly and slowly to her own truck.

Stephen was a bit envious that she was calling it a night, as Stephen couldn't. He went to the tool trailer and loaded up everything he'd need to clean up. Once that was through, he'd pour new cement—though a much thinner pad—over what they'd removed.

Moira was kind enough to let Stephen skate when he ambled in smelling like sweat and cement at a little after six in the morning. She did make him strip and wash his face and hands before he climbed into bed.

"Was it bad?" Moira asked, picking up Stephen's pants from the floor and retrieving his cellphone, his wallet, and a small stack of heavy old change.

"What?" Stephen said as he flopped onto the bed.

"The water thing."

"Oh, yeah, terrible. Had to cut cement and dig out..." he trailed, feigning the heavy breaths of sleep.

Moira set the contents of his pockets on the dresser and climbed back into bed after him. They'd have to be ready to go by eleven. They had to pick up Moira's new *best friend* Susan Hautala for Riley's funeral.

Stephen blinked at the slightly fatter than normal coins next to his wallet. If the burial was going to take, whatever it was—which he was fairly sure it would—he had no doubt the coins would disappear. He tried not to think about the fact he'd buried them with their rightful owner only hours earlier.

The day blew by in a blur. Five local men and a cousin of Riley's from Prince George carried the casket—the horribly light casket. The preacher talked and the mechanism lowered the box from view. Moira managed to unburden her shoulder, passing the Susan buck onto another woman from town. Rosemary hadn't shown up, which surprised most in attendance, but not Stephen. There was too much daylight and the people were too close together. No amount of makeup or fashion statements would cover the truth until the reversal started to kick in.

He napped when they got home and ate microwave popcorn for supper. His feet weren't itchy at all and he breathed a little easier.

It came almost as a surprise when Stephen saw the coins still on the dresser, still counting down by the day. He found he could ignore them if he tried, but now and then, Riley's face and Rosemary's skin popped to mind and he couldn't help but think about his feet and legs.

The words weren't fading, but the dry skin had ceased rising.

And there was Rosemary's humorless joke: *You got the quarter, could you spare me some change?* The words mirrored what was happening with an insight Stephen had refused to acknowledge, until they dug up the corpse, until they buried the man. Now that it was all over, he could work at relaxing, perhaps fall back into the tremendous stress of readying an entire apartment building on a ticking clock.

The following Tuesday he awoke with a dime and a nickel. He'd sent five text messages to Rosemary between Sunday and Monday, but she hadn't replied, so he decided to stop by her home. It was a little after seven when he parked behind her truck and went to the side of the home. The screen door was closed, but the wooden door was open about a foot inside.

"Rosemary? Rosemary, you home?" he said and pulled open the screen door. He shouted this time, "Hey! Rosemary!" He received no reply, but the home had a strange scent. Strange enough that he was curious and wee bit worried. "I'm coming in!"

His nose wrinkled and he took several quick sniffs as he crossed through a small laundry space, then a kitchen, and then to a hallway. He took a deep breath through his nose. It was car exhaust, but it was so completely out of place inside the home.

"Rosemary?" he said and leaned in to look at the living room. It was lived in, but not messy. "Hey, you home?"

He began sniffing again, following his nose like he was on the hunt for Fruit Loops. The hallway was dark, with carpeted floors and pale blue walls. There were no pictures or artistic accents. Everything was dull.

"Hey?" He stuck his head in through the first door and found the office. Cluttered, busy with papers and computer bric-a-brac, but empty otherwise. "Rosemary?" He found the bathroom next. A towel draped over the curtain rod, a shaggy blue mat on the floor by the tub, but no Rosemary. "Hey, Rosemary, where are you?" he said, but rather than go any further, he sent a text.

Two seconds later, her heard vibrating. He trailed the sound to a door at the end of the hall. He looked inside. There was a bed, sheets and blankets tossed and bundled, but no Rosemary. He stepped inside and saw the cellphone on the dresser next to a gun belt. The phone blinked at him.

"Rosemary, where the hell—?" He gasped.

On the floor, in a perverse imitation of the fetal position, was a bundle of splotchy silver and pink steel. It hit him almost instantly and he gasped again.

Rosemary's eyes flashed and her lips stretched, revealing a small chrome grill where her teeth had been. Brown saliva oozed around the fins of the grill.

"No...but we stopped it?" Stephen said and felt that itch, the one that maybe hadn't really gone away, but only migrated. He scratched at his neck absently. His eyes tight on the abomination huddled on the floor. "We did what you said would stop it!" he screamed suddenly.

Rosemary didn't appear to be listening. She was shifting her eyes to the left and flashing the blubs within.

"What?" Stephen said, voice rising to a whine. "What the hell am I supposed to do? You said it fixed it! You said you were feeling better!"

Rosemary kept shifting her eyes, as if pointing to the dresser.

"What, you want me to call someone? Who!" Stephen stared at her phone and then looked back at Rosemary. "What the fuck am I supposed to do?"

She kept flashing her eyes, and then he understood. She was pointing to the gun not the phone.

"Oh, no. No," Stephen said and took a step back.

Rosemary's eyes flared again and he reversed another step.

"I can't."

The boxy mass of metals began shaking and then rocking. Stephen froze, watching as a puff of exhaust filled the room and that scent he trailed into the home clouded around him like poisonous smog. Rosemary wasn't through. The rocking grew heavy enough that she tipped up, falling onto what would've been her knees and stomach. Her chin was an inch from the floor.

"What the fuck? What the fuck?" Stephen mumbled.

Before any understanding surfaced in his head, his body acted and leapt sideways, out of reach of the rocketing form coming at him. Rosemary crashed into the wall, sending plaster dust flying and puffing another cloud of smoke from her back end. She spun on the single wheel that had grown from her legs. She faced Stephen.

Stephen took a step left, Rosemary adjusted. He took two steps right, Rosemary adjusted. He took a step back and she rolled forward, brown fluid blowing hotly from her grill. Stephen jumped onto the bed to avoid it. From that vantage, he saw his chance and took it.

Two strides and he leapt off the bed and into the hallway. Rosemary spun behind him. He got two more steps before she melted carpet and burned rubber, nailing the backs of his legs, sending him to the ground. He yelped and then she was on top of him, spilling hot saliva—oil—over his neck and the back of his head.

Stephen cried out at the pain and shock, spinning sideways. Rosemary thunked heavily into the hallway wall. Stephen tried to roll out from beneath her, but she throttled her wheel against his side, bunching and tearing his shirt before raking into his flesh. He cried out again, but this time he flopped up and on top of her. His fingers wrapped around her cool steel neck and he began slamming her face into the floor.

Instantly, she ceased fighting, but Stephen was on a roll. He slammed and slammed until hot fluid puddled around them while steel clanked and crinkled, smoke barrelled free of her tailpipe in great puffs. She wasn't moving and wasn't revving or flashing.

He rolled off her to lay on his back, exhausted and overwrought.

"You said that would do it. The water and the proper burial, you said."

Rosemary's eyes flashed and from deep, deep within the hollow drum of her core she said, "Shoot...me."

Stephen had only ever shot one handgun in his life up to that point. It was orange and grey, had a long black cord and the word Zapper on the butt. Rosemary's service pistol was very unlike the Nintendo controller. It was heavy and cold and felt ugly in his grip.

He'd used a pillow like they did in movies, but it didn't muffle as much of the sound as he'd hoped. Still, it kept the oil splash back to a minimum and saved his hearing some. Her eyes no longer shined or moved. He watched her as he wiped his prints from the gun, wondering how did one wipe the gun's prints from his hands. He stumbled to the living room and sat for a moment, unthinking of who might've heard the shot, his screams, and called it in, but simply catching his breath. His life had gone utterly nuts over the last two weeks and he didn't know how or if there was any way back.

How would his wife live without him?

Who would his son grow up to be without a father?

Who would finish the apartments and take the burden off his family when he inevitably...what?

Turned into a book?

He cradled his chin in his hands and let his eyes fall to the coffee table. There was a manila folder open with a note and three 8x10 photographs on it. The note read: *Here's the shots of the guy who passed through a couple weeks ago. Did he make it up your way? Is he causing trouble?* The photographs were of the man he'd helped bury. The man who'd become bones. The man who'd cursed them.

Stephen got moving. He didn't want to have to explain anything, especially not the mechanical woman dead in the hallway.

He was barely around a corner when a police cruiser pulled into Rosemary's laneway. He nailed the accelerator to the floor and steered. Mind elsewhere, he found himself almost one hundred miles from home, eating a cheeseburger in a diner, thinking Ruthie's did it better, and then thinking of Sonya.

She'd spoken to the guy, at least a little.

Stephen wiped his face and left cash on the table, and just to see, left behind the two American coins. He waited in the lot a moment, saw the waitress pick up the coins, and then reached into his left pocket where he'd kept the change separate. Empty. He withdrew his wallet and then fished for coins.

He brought his hand up and came back a nickel and four pennies.

"No," he whispered.

He looked through the window at the waitress taking an order. His hand slammed back into his pocket, feeling folds and lint, the stiffness at the seam, and then, as if toying with him, he located the missing coin.

"I did what I had to!" he shouted and threw the change at the dash of his truck. "Don't you see? It wasn't my fault! I did what I had to do!" He wrenched against the wheel in a short-lived tantrum.

The entire trip, his phone vibrated. Panting, feeling ready to burst, he answered. Four missed calls in the last twenty minutes from an unknown number, and one from the man he'd hired to finish the apartments. He opened his texts. That same man said the light fixtures, switch covers, closet doors, and bathroom mirrors had arrived, and that the delivery man had been calling Stephen, needing a signature. Stephen texted him back and then dialed the number who'd called him four times.

Work, like refuge from the storm, had Stephen calming, and for a short while, he wasn't thinking about the curse at all…until he itched the back of his head and hair fell down to his shoulders. His fingers played over the soft bald spot, imagining he could see the words that were surely there.

"Sonya," he said, and floored the gas pedal.

"I already sold the coins. Mailed them on Friday, sorry."

Stephen had on a Vancouver Canucks ball cap and a flannel shirt with a deep collar. He forced a smile. "Yeah, I was more curious about the man."

"Why?" Sonya sat at the rearmost table of Ruthie's. It was a quarter to five and she'd been rolling silverware into napkins for fifteen minutes and would continue to do so until the first real customer came in for supper.

"Uh, curious. I don't know, I like coins." Stephen stumbled, it sounded like bullshit even to him.

"Was it like the books? Did your dad collect coins, too?" Sonya said, frowning.

"That's exactly right!"

"Oh, and you think he'll have more?"

"Sure, maybe."

"He was hitchhiking? I doubt he has a coin collection on him."

"No, of course not," Stephen said, thinking *he only had three coins when we buried him the first time.*

"So what?"

"Maybe he's a rich eccentric."

"Hey, yeah. Maybe. Could be. I saw a guy like that on an *Unsolved Mysteries* re-run. Guy went around leaving huge tips and then vanished."

"See, so maybe he only looks bummy."

"Real far from home, though. Said he was from Alabama and his family was from there, too. Near that town with the KKK bridge. You know, that bridge where the Black people marched. I saw that on A and E." Sonya snapped her fingers trying to jog a memory.

"Did he say—?"

"Selma! From near Selma."

"He say where exactly?"

"No, but he made it seem like it wasn't too far from Selma, but maybe I imagined that."

Stephen tapped on the table, thinking, gazing vacantly through the cook's window across the counter.

"Sure you don't want a coffee, just brewed it. You look a little frazzled."

"Yeah, okay."

"You're home early." Paul said. He smelled like fresh-cut grass and gasoline—he worked summer maintenance at the local poultry plant.

"Yeah, I, uh, yeah." Stephen sat at the family desktop, the Google search bar blinking its cursor and three tabs open to pages dedicated to Selma, Alabama. One more open to Google Maps.

"You, *uh, yeah,* what?"

"Oh, I...is there a way to search faces on Google? Pictures of people, I mean?"

"Only if they post enough pictures. It mostly works with celebrities and stolen memes."

Stephen opened the folder and tapped the top and best photo of the mysterious man. "Can you do it with that one?"

"Who is it?"

"Some guy, don't worry about it."

Paul leaned over the picture with his cellphone out. "He steal something from the site?"

"I said don't worry about it."

"Fine." Paul typed into his phone and within ten seconds gave the answer. "Nope. He's not on social media or anywhere else Google searches."

Stephen let his head fall into his hands, revealing the bald patch on the back of his scalp to his son.

"You get a tattoo?" Paul said, pitch high as a question could take it.

"What? Oh, no." Stephen put his hand over the spot. He suddenly wondered if he could tell his son, work out the mystery as a father-son team, like an Ellery Queen mystery. But no. "You should shower before supper."

Paul made a theatrical show of smelling his armpits. "Probably," he said and started away. He stopped at his bedroom door. "I guess we could try Reddit, but it probably won't help."

"Oh," Stephen said as he scratched absently at the back of his head, sending lazy hairs to his shoulders and big flakes of dandruff.

"Are you sick?" Moira asked him after he came out of the bathroom with a towel wrapped around his suddenly bald head.

He flicked the light switch off. "I...I guess I am," he said and lay down on the bed next to his wife.

"Is it stress or something more...?" she trailed, letting notions of the big C dangle like an invisible carrot.

Stephen was on his side and pulled the towel from his head. He looked at the change pile, waiting for the next penny to disappear.

"What are those words?" Moira said and reached out to touch him.

He jerked away. "Better not."

"Better not what? What in the hell is happening here, Stephen?" Venom and terror made up the underlining cocktail of her mood.

The antlers jutting from Riley's forehead. The light covers Rosemary had for eyes. Those images mingled and he tried to imagine how a man could become a book. Was it truly inevitable? They'd reburied the corpse in consecrated ground, which should've worked. He'd searched Google for the man, and didn't stop at the image—he'd typed hitchhiker and Alabama and old coins, and fifteen shades of all that together, but it didn't help.

"Goddammit! Talk to me!"

Stephen cringed, but couldn't muster the will to say it.

Moira grabbed onto Stephen's shoulder and tried to turn him around to face her, but jerked her hand away in pain. "Ouch!"

Stephen couldn't help but to turn. Moira had her right index finger in her mouth. "What?" he said.

"Cut me." Moira spoke around her finger.

Stephen touched his shoulder where she had and felt something like onion skin fins. He closed his eyes. She'd gotten a papercut, simply by touching him the wrong way. She'd gotten a papercut and there were still seven days and a handful of hours left in the change—like a payphone call.

Stephen sighed. "Riley and Rosemary were having an affair."

Moira stopped fussing with her finger and listened.

"They'd been out drinking at Riley's cabin and on their way back to town, they ran down a dirty hitchhiker." Stephen scratched behind his ear, working the edges of a scab free. "They called me to help them get rid of the body. We buried it in the boiler room at the site, in the sump pump gulley. Rosemary gave us each one of the dead man's coins, to remind us we were all in it together."

"What the fuck? Why would you help them?" Moira was audibly indignant, but hardly moved her body.

"Our livelihoods are tied to Riley and Rosemary. If they went to court, the funding would dry up. The apartment building would never get finished. We lose our home!"

"Riley's dead though..." Moira trailed off. Being dead wouldn't cost any outrageous lawyer fees or taint a business investment like a drunken hit and run. She sniffled. "Okay, but...he was a person, what about his family?"

"It all just happened too fast. But that's only part of it. You didn't see Riley's body. Moira, he'd turned into a deer. Not in shape so much, but his skin was a pelt and he had antlers. Christ, his jaw was all deformed."

Moira gasped then. "I thought she was crazy," she whispered. "Susan, I told her to see a psychiatrist because she was hallucinating. I think that's why she picked someone else to lean on. I thought I'd weaselled away, but she picked someone else."

Stephen paused to lick his lips, thanks to a bedraggled widow, this was going better than he'd assumed. "Riley got the nickel from the man's change. Rosemary got the dime. Tomorrow, if it's not out already, news of Chief Rosemary Young's death is going to be the new hot topic around town. They'll probably say unknown illness or suspicious circumstances."

"No."

"Yes. She turned into a fucking bastardized car. Her eyes were light covers and they glowed red. She grew a wheel...she attacked me, trying to get me to kill her," Stephen took a deep breath through his nose, "and I did. I killed her. I had to."

Moira reached out for Stephen but stopped short of touching him.

"I got the quarter and every damned day the amount has been shrinking."

"What?" Moira retracted her hand and pressed it to her chest.

"I'm down to eight cents. Tomorrow morning it will be seven and I'll be a little more made of words and paper."

"What does that mean?"

Stephen paused again, gathering himself. He'd never been so terrified of words, especially not of words coming out of his mouth. "The man cursed us and we're turning into something we love. I'm becoming my father's book collection, or a version of it. I have words all over my feet and now my head. Tomorrow they'll probably start up my back, maybe even on my dick and balls."

It was Moira's turn for silence. She lit the bedside lamp and took a hard, hard look at the man she'd married. She burst into tears. "How do we stop it?"

"I don't know. We already dug up the body and planted it in the cemetery on Wakefield, behind that old church. Rosemary had his picture—a cop from a station down south snapped his shot when the man was passing through. I know his family was from somewhere near Selma, Alabama, but that's it."

"How does any of that help?"

Stephen let the words of an unexplored thought pass through his lips. "I want to take the body—just a skeleton now—down there and see if I can't find out more about the man. I mean, if he's been hitchhiking, maybe someone's seen him. The pictures are clear and...shit, I don't know."

Moira didn't miss a step. "Should we leave now? We'll have to drive, never get a corpse on a plane."

"Only a skeleton now, somehow, but yeah." Stephen kicked out from the bed, the thrumming terror dishing out adrenaline like Halloween candy on an endless October night.

They were in a short line to cross from Chopaka, British Columbia into Nighthawk, Washington by the time Paul struggled from bed and found the note on the counter. They'd kept it vague and light, calling it a spur of the moment vacation.

He blinked at it and then at the ringing business line in the office. He shuffled absently and leaned in to see the caller ID.

"Police?" Suddenly certain there'd been an accident. "Hello?" he said after putting the receiver to his cheek.

"Stephen Barber?" The voice belonged to a man, and a large one by the sound of it.

"No. I'm Paul. My dad's Stephen." Knowing there hadn't been an accident did not lessen the adrenaline thrum riding his veins.

"Stephen home?"

"No, Dad and Mom went on a vacation."

The man clucked his tongue. "That right?"

Paul said nothing to this, listened to the man's breathing while tightening his grip.

"They have cellphones?"

"Sure," Paul said and then gave the numbers.

The bones were in a large suitcase in the backseat, buried in old clothes. The Barbers had packed two other cases and printed out a phony itinerary, including hotels, national parks, and a few tourist hotspots. The guard spied the list for a long time and then handed it back, saying only, "If you get time on your way home, head into Seattle, the gum wall is real interesting."

"Okay," Moira said.

She'd taken over driving after Stephen needed a break to rub lotion anywhere that was trying to flake. She put her sunglasses back on and headed southeast. They had about forty more hours to cover. On the dash, a nickel and two pennies jingled a tuneless rhythm.

Stephen tried to sleep but couldn't. According to his phone, he'd missed two calls, and after listening to the messages, decided the cops back home could wait. Also, what in the hell would he say about either of his business partners? He got back behind the wheel at a McDonald's on the eastern outskirts of Spokane. Moira suggested the burgers were greasier here and then fell asleep. They'd been on the road seven hours and the afternoon sun blazed behind them. A little after six o'clock, Stephen pulled over in Deer Lake, Montana for gas and grub. This time he passed out after eating a submarine sandwich and Moira kept the truck rolling.

Stephen awoke to find Moira had parked in a truck stop lot and was snoozing next to him. She sat up with a start when he tried to stretch his legs.

"Where are we?" he asked.

"I was just resting my eyes a minute—last place was called Colony, I think. We're in Wyoming. I had to rest my eyes a minute, that's all," she spoke through a sleepy fog.

On the dash were a nickel and a penny. Meaning he'd been sleeping a good long while. "I'll take over, but will you run in for some food and coffee? People will stare at me." Stephen had added the second part softly.

Moira only nodded and hopped out of the truck.

Five pit stops and two turns at the wheel each, they reached the southern end of Memphis, Tennessee and pulled into a crummy looking joint with no name. The word MOTEL in thirty-foot letters sat atop the squat forty-two-unit establishment. Moira stepped inside and up to the desk. The young man took down her name on a laptop and copied her driver's license.

"Room twelve. Key's in the door," he said.

"What?" Moira was moments from crashing and something wasn't quite computing.

"Key's in the door. Leave the key on the dresser when you leave, or bring it inside."

"What?"

"The key's in the lock on your door. All the unoccupied rooms have keys in the doors. Take the key into the room with you."

Moira shook her head gently, unable to comprehend, but unable to converse any further. She turned and left with only her receipt and the knowledge that she'd rented room twelve for sixty-five American bucks.

She climbed into the truck and Stephen said, "They leave all the keys in the doors, look."

She looked and finally understood, but it offered a new question. "We're in twelve. How do they keep people from...?" she trailed. They were a decent trek from the city and going all that way just to squat in some raggedy old motel didn't make any sense, so there was her answer.

"I guess it's the honor system." Stephen parked in front of the door. He yawned and the back of his throat vibrated like rustling paper in the wind.

The sleeps were deep, but brief. Minutes after the noon hour, they were in Selma and suddenly didn't know where to go. They drove the streets, crossed the Edmund Pettus Bridge four times, and finally veered onto the main drag. It was just a town. Its far-reaching infamy made it seem as if it would be bigger, a place with countless rocks to overturn. But no.

"Where do we start?" Stephen asked. That morning he'd pocketed a nickel and a penny as he studied lines from *Moby Dick* across his stomach. He only recognized it for Queequeg's dialogue–not many books with a character named Queequeg–before pulling his shirt the rest of the way down.

"There's a café up there. Guess we could show the picture around."

Stephen was certain she'd said *we* with intent. Embarrassed or not, looking strange or not, he had to join her and push for answers. He pulled out onto the street and parked almost directly in front of the Blooming Rose.

Inside smelled like coffee and fryer grease. A few patrons sat at the counter while a waitress filled mugs with coffee from a pot and a cook slid two hearty looking plates along a counter. Stephen quickly overcame his discomfort over the writing on his head and neck and felt something foreign and enlightening.

In Shiny River, a town about half the size of Selma, there was one Black family–a husband, wife, and daughter. Everywhere they went in

Shiny River, chances were, they were the only Black people there. Stephen had never considered it or wondered how that felt until he moseyed up behind the stool next to his wife, the only white peas in that particular pod of Black faces. He immediately wondered how tense things were in town. They'd been tense there before, certainly, but were they still? Did the recent protests touch this rundown place?

Suddenly, Stephen wanted to apologize for white people in general, but Moira saved him the embarrassment. "Can we get a couple coffees, please?" she said and sat on a padded stool at the lunch counter.

Stephen fell in next to her and tapped the manila envelope gently with the index finger of his right hand.

"Did all that hurt, on your head that way?" an old man asked from the end of the counter. "I got a tattoo in Vietnam and never got another, stung for real for real."

Stephen had played a version of this conversation through his mind a half-dozen times already that morning alone. "Not too bad. Some spots where it's close to bone."

The waitress came by with the coffeepot. "Where y'all from?"

"British Columbia, Canada."

"That right? What you doing down here?"

Moira pulled the manila folder out from beneath Stephen's hand and flipped it open. "We're looking for this man."

The waitress gave a sidelong look at the photograph and then adjusted, drank it in full on. "He's a dirty one. He from 'round here?"

"Said he was. He was up in Canada and we lost track of him. He was hitchhiking. You have a lot of hitchhikers around here?" Moira asked.

"No, ma'am. You bounty hunters?" the waitress asked.

Stephen dressed his coffee and had to grin around the cup before he took a sip. "No, but he was an interesting fellow and said he was from down near here. He had some valuable coins and we're collectors, thought maybe while we were on vacation down this way, that we'd take a look around for him."

"Uh huh?" the waitress said and sounded about one percent convinced. "Hey, Leroy, take a look at this dirty white man in the pictures."

The cook stepped out from the back. He was a big man with big arms and short legs. He looked at the best of the photos for a couple seconds, then shook his head and returned to his kitchen.

"Pass them on down here," the man said at the end of the counter.

Stephen stood and tipped a bit funny, the big toe of his right foot had gone numb. He walked on the ball of his foot and carted the envelope to show the man with only one tattoo.

The man sucked around his dentures, flipping through the shots, and then pouted out his lips. "Can't say he looks like someone I'd know. You say he's got valuable coins? For real for real?"

"I bought some from him," Stephen said, and he guessed right then that he wasn't lying. He'd bought and paid for the coins the man had given out. Would pay a little more yet.

The four other patrons each took a look at the photos, but all apologized at the lack of recognition. Moira nodded at each and then paid for the coffees. "Any ideas where we might ask?"

"Pardon me, but your fella here looks a bit...a bit like a bum. Might be smart to check in at the library. If he was actually holding anything valuable and still dresses like that, could be he's one of those old money types who's cheap as all get out." The waitress accepted the five one-dollar bills for the coffee and smiled courteously when she offered change and Moira waved it off. "I hope you find him."

"Me too," Stephen said and led the way out of the café.

Outside, Moira said, "Your foot hurt?"

"I can't feel my big toe... Don't worry about it, let's find the library." Stephen pulled his phone out as he spoke and did a very quick search in Google. "Next phone bill will be outrageous, eh?"

Moira said nothing to that.

The library, while pleasant, was another bust. The librarian sent the Barbers to Lannie's B-B-Q. The cook there sent the Barbers to Hancock's Barbeque. The head waitress sent them then to Michael's Pub, out of town a ways.

Loaded with meat and potatoes, Stephen limped in the lead and stepped into Michael's.

It was a small sports bar lost somewhere in time. Old men sat around a stained and chipped bar sipping drinks with their heads craned to see the TV screen—a retro Michael Eubanks fight airing on ESPN.

Stephen ordered a Budweiser and Moira ordered a mojito. The bartender, a middle-aged white man with a potbelly and sandy blonde hair, grinned at this, as if she'd challenged him. And perhaps she had, in a way.

The pictures came out and the men were more worried why they were looking for the man than in potentially recognizing him. They stuck to the story about the coins and it seemed to carry enough weight to impress.

"You ought to check in at the flea market. I seen some guys selling coins there before," said a man from somewhere along the line of men, his eyes back on the Eubanks rerun.

Stephen looked at Moira and sighed, puffing out his lips. They'd burned the day and he didn't have any days to burn.

They headed out and back into Selma proper. According to Google, the Selma Hotel was the cheapest stay and they checked in, explaining they'd be there for no more than five days, hopefully fewer. Moira didn't bother showing the photographs and Stephen didn't bother stepping to the desk with her.

They climbed into bed and lay on the starchy sheets, farting away road food. Moira laughed and cried, and then snored in the gentle way she always had. Stephen laughed a little and ran his toe against the bed and stayed up too late thinking about life and if there was any way forward, and another missed call from the police back home. He kept his eyes on the coins. At four minutes after four, the glint of the coins beneath the moonlight changed shade.

The penny had disappeared.

Jo Bradner had grey hair down her back with three small braids woven amid the loose strands. Each braid sported six leather ties of a variety of colors. She had a ball piercing through the meat of her left cheek and hoops that stretched her earlobes in way that only ever seemed normal within the pages of National Geographic. She had pale blue eyes and the long years of her life had dried and thinned her lips to a state of near non-existence.

She spoke with little accent and total certainty. "I have seen this man. These pictures are enhanced?" The way she said it made clear she was leading somewhere.

"I don't think so. Why?" Stephen said, liking how this woman didn't stare at him, though he'd awoken from a brief sleep with a swatch of dead skin on his pillow big enough to wrap a can of beans, and fresh lettering continuing nearly all the way around his neck.

Jo shook her head gently. "Has to be, unless…" she trailed and looked over her shoulder to her partner in the sales of vintage collectables. "I'm going to talk to these people for a few minutes." The old man waved from his rocking chair. The flea market wasn't all that busy and nobody had stopped by the Bradner table the entire time Stephen and Moira stood there. "Come with me, I need a smoke."

Stephen and Moira followed the woman through a set of side doors that led from the market floor to a picnic table parked on a small swatch of weedy grass.

"Be right back," Jo said to the Barbers and then walked backwards toward a secondary parking lot. "You want cokes?"

"Sure," Moira said.

"Yeah, thanks," Stephen said.

Jo turned back around and opened the rear door of a big, brown panel van. Seconds later she carried three jars of fizzy black liquid sealed beneath gold tinted lids.

"Olivier makes the coke with a hint of blackberry juice." Jo set the drinks down and retrieved a steel cigarette case—vintage, silver—and pulled out a roll-your-own cigarette. "I'd offer a smoke, but..." she trailed again before pointing to the jars. "It's good, I promise."

Stephen twisted the cap off a jar after he got himself situated on the picnic table—his right leg from the knee down had joined his toe in numbness. He took a mouthful. It was too sweet for his taste, but he took a second mouthful for show.

Moira tapped the top photograph. "Tell us about him."

Jo sucked a heavy drag that crackled and sent orange embers scattering, and exhaled a big cloud with a slight after tang of marijuana amid heavy tobacco notes. "This memory's clear as day, probably I don't remember any single scene in my life like I remember this one." She stabbed the two fingers holding her cigarette at the top image. "That face has stuck with me and I couldn't forget it even if I tried."

The river ran high and lazy at the fat spot where the land spread apart, as if welcoming kids on their summer breaks. Rebecca Crowder had on a one-piece with a blue mid-section and a ruffled white bottom. Accenting her waist was a phony red belt. On her right breastbone was a small anchor and rope done in gold thread. The idea was that she looked like a sailor.

Three of the girls mooned over the terrific swimsuit and the two boys in attendance wagged their tongues and panted like dogs in heat. Ten-year-old Jo Bradner did not moon over the outfit, she couldn't even look at it because it was so groovy and cool, and made her tank top and mismatching shorts look downright foolish, made her look like she had no fashion sense at all. The truth of it was that her father was painfully cheap and didn't allow her nice things if they increased the purchase price.

Jo stayed away from the group milling around Rebecca and in the shade by the edge of the river where it slimmed out and fish passed by with regularity. She sometimes imagined dropping in a hook, how the boys did, but didn't dare because those same boys would make fun of her and the girls would pinch the fat on her thighs and love handles.

Grace and Kirk Hunter's sister, Lana, was supposed to be watching them. Lana was seventeen, usually smelled like Oh! de London by Yardley, wore too much lipstick, and had a rep. A Chevrolet Bel-Air pulled to a stop on the road above and a boy started shouting for Lana.

"You don't tell Mom or Dad or I'll bust your heads," Lana said, sneering at her siblings.

Everyone, aside from Jo, laughed and made jokes about Lana and when she'd have to go live with an aunt because some boy would slip her some action with no intention of slipping her a ring. Only minutes had passed sans their chaperone before an old truck parked on the road above and a man in a suit came down the hill, bouncing from rock to rock like he'd been there before.

"Who wants a Coke?" the man said.

He was short and pale, had on a fine grey suit, black loafers, and a gold watch. His hair was thin down the middle and thick at the sides. Shadows played beneath his armpits and sweat dripped along his face. It was warm, but not quite that warm—which was why the kids had stayed out of the river. He had small box between his hands.

Jo slunk deep into the trees and watched.

The other kids stood around the man, drinking from bottles. None had drank much beyond the necks when they started to go woozy. The man took out a short knife and stabbed Kirk in the face and neck. He then stabbed the other boy before he had a chance to run. The girls spun away, but all were dopey and two fell—Rebecca being one of them. The man chased the two runners and stabbed them in the back, hard enough to spray fantastic swatches of red about the brown sand of the shore. He pounced on Grace. She was the first to fall and the first to try to scream for help.

Only Rebecca was left, and she started begging as the man started stripping away his pants. He was down over her, between her thighs. He tore her wonderful bathing suit away and she screamed, "Help me, Jo!" and reached a hapless hand out to where Jo had hidden. The man turned and spotted her amidst the greens and browns. The only way out was down the river or up the bank, and she chose poorly.

She broke for the stones that led to the road and the man stabbed Rebecca in the chest twice before trailing behind Jo, reefing his pants up. She took the first and second and third rock, only one more before she could maybe put her hands around the guardrail post, which was only a couple feet from her bicycle, when the knife burned hot into her side. The man grabbed her by the hair and she screamed for help. He tossed her to the blood-stained ground and cut away her clothes with two deft swipes with the small blade. She punched him and he stabbed her in the chest. The air grew cold and difficult to handle, her right lung filling up with blood.

"I'm gonna fuck you so go—" That was as far as he got.

A shadow came as if out of nowhere and a rock nailed her attacker in the head. He fell sideways. Jo was almost out, but the image of a bearded man appeared before her like a devil from the sky—the scrambling footfalls of the attacker carrying off into midafternoon air. The bearded man looked disgusting—filthy, ragged, destitute—and dragged her body over next to Rebecca—who was still laboring for breath—and pressed his hands over the worst of both girls' wounds. His voice carried like an ambulance siren. "Help! These kids been stabbed!" He then put his face down between Jo and Rebecca and whispered. "Help's coming. This time, help's coming. This time I'll get the help."

The man was crying into the bloody sand and Jo watched him, understanding that he wasn't a devil, but an angel.

"I'll never forget his face. Even the clothes look the same," Jo said. She was onto her fourth cigarette.

Forgetting the point for a moment, Moira asked, "Did they catch the other guy?"

Jo shook her head. "Some cops tried to pin it on the man, but Rebecca and me cleared him. I guess there were plenty of footprints from the other guy, too. He had small feet. So they had to let the man with the beard go. Nobody ever heard from him again."

"That was here, in Selma?" Stephen asked.

"No, that was just outside of Blueville, on Slow Hills Road." Jo stubbed her cigarette out on the leg of the picnic table and pocketed the butt. "About an hour southeast of here."

"Do you think anybody else would recognize him?" Moira said.

"Best check in at the Advocate. Not too many towns kept their paper going, but Blueville has. Google will tell you where, I'm sure."

"You said the attack took place in 'sixty-five?" Moira said.

"That's right. I was ten. Grace Hunter was the oldest. She was twelve. Most of us were eleven, but I was only ten and kind of just followed along because they were from the same neighborhood I was from, but one of their uncles showed them the swimming spot and we used to take our bikes out there." Jo pushed sideways, making ready to stand up. "I'd better get back in there, Olivier'll think I went to the john and fell in."

No need to stay in Selma any longer, they checked out of the room and hit the road. The editor at the Blueville Advocate only knew vaguely of the slaughter on the riverbank, but said he'd pass on their contact to the retired editor. He also suggested they visit the library, maybe dust off some microfiche.

"You doing a podcast or something?"

Moira agreed because it sounded better than any alternative.

When she hung up, she looked at Stephen behind the wheel. "It's a lead, anyway."

"I can't feel much of my leg, so that lead better call us soon." Stephen said, and two minutes of silence mounted between them before he added, "I buried an angel. That woman called him an angel and maybe she was right."

"If it's the same guy and not a relative."

"It's him."

"Yeah, I think so, too." Moira reached over to rub Stephen's shoulder.

The librarian's assistant was almost gleeful to help with the microfiche trays and explaining how the machine worked. "I've never heard of this one, but the whole state has such a storied past," she said. "I'm actually from Minnesota, but it's too danged cold up there, and Blueville had an opening. Well, you probably know how it goes. You're from Canada, right?"

Moira cocked her head sideways. "How'd you figure that out?"

"You talk like Canadians. I had a boyfriend from Alberta once. He said *eh* all the time, so now whenever I hear it, I listen up. Y'all only said it twice, but you sure don't sound American, so I put it together with the fact you said you'd come a long ways."

"I hadn't noticed I'd said it," Moira said.

"Me neither."

"You did."

"Okay, so, which one has summer, nineteen-sixty-five in it?" Stephen said from where he sat. His right leg had begun to give him real trouble.

"Should be this—" The assistant craned her neck at a voice coming from beyond the doorway of what might've been called the ancient technologies room. "Just a minute!" Her hands worked at loading the carousel into the machine, not exactly deftly, but obviously she'd done it before, if sparingly. "Load them like that and make sure they go back into the right boxes when you're done."

"Thanks," Stephen said, his left hand hovered above the wheel that turned the frames.

"Cool tattoo, by the way," the librarian's assistant said as she hurried away.

The light tone of her presence carried any easiness from the musty, dusty room at the back of the library when she left. Stephen started bouncing and rolling over stories, fast enough that Moira only caught the first word of two from a headline—Stephen was simply looking for pictures.

"Slow down, you might miss something."

Stephen sneered. "It'll be a story with a headline and a picture."

"Yeah, but..." Moira trailed.

The tenseness was palpable and the first carousel took almost two hours to search at Moira's suggested speed. Stephen popped in the next and only had to go a short way until they were into September, 1965.

"Can you go back? I think I saw something," Moira said.

Stephen pushed back in the chair and stomped part of the way across the room, moving almost peg-legged, and then pulled out a padded chair. He sat and cradled his head. "I did something horrible and I'm going to die a freak because of it."

Moira opened her mouth, but closed it and took over the wheel. She bumped along slowly until she hit the thing Stephen had passed by. It was a follow-up story, from August 25, 1965.

THE WALKING SON – UPDATE

The man who called himself Lewis and who the public has dubbed 'The Walking Son' is still but a mystery, and that mystery is getting deeper. We've been talking to locals who had seen his picture when we first ran it in May, and it seems a few had seen him before.

"I know that face anywhere, scared the bejesus out of me, Lord," said Gwen Harding of Point Line Road, Blueville. "I'd say it was his father if I was worried about being called silly, but I'm too old for that. Me and Teddy, rest his soul, picked this man off the side of the road in 1922. I told Teddy to keep on driving, but Teddy told me to hush because a man in need is a man in need. Well, he was real quiet, said he was from around, but was vague on the particulars. I swear by our true God in Heaven, it was the same man you printed in the paper. He even showed us a picture of his mama."

The police had been vague themselves when the story first came out, as they assumed he was the criminal who had murdered and defiled those poor children. I called Chief Abell of the Blueville PD and asked if the man calling himself Lewis had anything in his wallet. Being as the man had been cleared, Chief Abell was more forthcoming. He said the man had some change and a picture of his mother, but nothing else.

"I would've gotten his name eventually, but someone here got a little hasty with opening cells once he was cleared of wrongdoing," said Chief Abell. "I suspect, had we held him a little longer, we would've gotten his full name and the mayor would've given him a key to the town."

Moira turned and called Stephen over. "You have to read this. Did he have a picture of his mother in his wallet?"

Stephen gasped. He'd forgotten all about the foggy photograph. It was a woman, older, but it had no markings and seemed like something discarded, then found and kept for interest sake. "Yes. Yes," he said, hissing the S sounds.

"It happened in May. That Jo woman must've gotten the date wrong." Moira stood from the chair closest to the machine and dug into the box of carousels until she found the right one.

"We're closing in five minutes and I need to put this stuff away." The librarian's assistant had much of her pep sucked from her step. She looked tired. "Did you find what you were looking for?"

Moira pulled out her cellphone and snapped shots of the screen to reread once they got back to their hotel room. They had a name to go on with a reasonable ruse to carry their questions.

"Do you know anything about The Walking Son?" Stephen asked, his throat was parched and his belly grumbled fiercely.

"Can't say I do," the assistant said and packed up the box. "You can always come back Monday to keep looking. We're closed tomorrow."

"Do you know any old locals who might know about The Walking Son?" Moira asked, it wouldn't do to waste a day.

"Sorry," the woman said as she left view down a dim hallway.

"What now?" Moira said.

"Supper, I suppose." Stephen pushed to his feet. "The left one's getting numb now, too."

They found a Mexican place and asked the staff if they'd heard of The Walking Son and then showed the photograph. It was negative all around, aside from the great food. They rented a room at the cheapest motel in town. It had a balcony and Moira and Stephen sat outside, drinking beer and combing through unrelated Google findings while hooked onto the Wi-Fi.

Stephen found The Walking Son had been mentioned in a top twenty American mysteries video, but the subject lasted all of two minutes and gave them nothing new, suggesting perhaps the man was a time traveller.

"I guess we have to hope that newspaper man calls, huh?" Moira said.

Stephen sighed and slipped his socks off. His right leg was parchment white aside from the words. He scratched at an itchy spot and found the surface of his skin had give, moving as if he'd grown tiny fins. Like the edge of a well-worn book.

"We're going to figure this out," Moira said, she had her pant legs rolled up and her shirt unbuttoned to the clasp of her bra.

Blueville, Alabama was hot and it was damp, making the watery beer nicer than it ought to be. Stephen reached for a fifth and cracked it.

He took a mouthful and then held the can to his forehead.

"There's life insurance. It covers the site, the house, and two years of my income. That's how the guy figured it." Stephen wasn't looking at Moira, but instead at the steady flow of traffic on the highway not thirty yards away. "So you and Paul, you'll be okay."

Moira took a shuddering breath through her mouth and exhaled from her nose. "Shut the fuck up, Stephen. Just shut the fuck up. We didn't come all this way to give up. You still have time."

Stephen pulled the heavy nickel from his pocket and studied it. "The Walking Son, an angel, a bag of bones. You should've seen Rosemary. It was the most awful thing I think I've ever seen. She was so far from human, but I could still see her in there, in all that metal."

"Do you think she would've lived long, if you didn't shoot her?"

Stephen shook his head gently. "I hope not. Even after what happened and her part in it...fuck, just think if I'd never teamed up with them. Imagine if I'd have waited a little longer, figured some other way to raise the capital."

"Stephen. Don't. You know someone would've been in there sooner than later. It's our future and it's going to work out, so just stop."

Stephen set down his beer and picked up his phone—no more missed calls, thank god. He did a quick search of Rosemary Young and found the official statement was suicide and that she'd suffered from an undisclosed illness. They weren't digging into what had taken them to the scene. Which was a little bit comforting, though not very.

"Let's sit in the air-conditioning, eh?" Moira put a firm hand on his shoulder, but didn't rub, as if worried about another papercut.

Together they spooned on the queen size bed, *Dr. Pimple Popper* on the tube, the lights out, and the TV remote within easy reach.

"Wonder what she'd think of my skin."

Moira kissed his still very Stephen cheek. "Probably not much. She's in it for the goo."

"This is the most disgusting show I've ever seen."

"But it's impossible to look away."

"Yeah. I guess." Stephen took a deep breath. "What if we find out where the body goes or whatever and stop it, but I'm stuck like this?"

"Stephen."

"No, really. What happens then?"

"I don't know, but you'll still be you."

"Almost."

"No, listen. You talk about insurance and me and Paul being okay, and it's not true. We wouldn't be okay. We're a trio, and soon enough Paul will be off on his own. So without you, it's only me, and that's not okay. It's not okay!"

Stephen turned his face far enough around to kiss Moira's mouth. "It's the same as if I got in a bad accident or got sick...I am sick. Pretend this is cancer if it makes it easier."

"No. No. No!" Moira grabbed him and flipped him onto his back. They'd gone to bed in their underwear and were immediately on the floor. "You're not dying, goddammit!" She grabbed him where he was still all man and squeezed and tugged until he stiffed.

"Okay," Stephen whispered.

Moira mounted him and Stephen turned off *Dr. Pimple Popper.*

Four pennies sat on the dresser next to Stephen's wallet.

The morning became afternoon became evening, Stephen's phone refused to ring and Moira had only received a pair of texts from Paul.

After fighting with a subdued appetite, Stephen rose from the bed to visit the can and dropped in a heap. It did not hurt, but what he saw made him scream.

His tibia and the tarsals of his feet had become spines to the pages of paper-muscle, -tendons, -veins, -arteries, and -flesh of his right leg. As he moved, the pages fanned like an especially fat phonebook.

"Okay. Okay," Moira said and dropped to her knees, putting her hands on the pages, as if holding the leg shape made it possible to pretend there was more time.

"Hello, I'm looking for Stephen Barber. He wanted to know about the murders back in 'sixty-five?" The voice was gruff and raspy.

"I'm his wife and we're working together on this," Moira said, bubbling, shooting to her feet.

When they'd awoken that morning, Stephen had those four pennies next to his wallet, both legs below the knees were loose books, and he could no longer hold a conversation—only push short, papery responses. His lips and eyelids were peeling endless flaky swatches. Words had begun parading over his arms. His neck to thighs had only line space gaps between the dark prose. Much of his face remained as of yet unblemished.

"We're more looking for informa—"

"You have to call me back. This number's long distance and I don't have a plan that covers long distance."

Moira checked the call display, but he'd already hung up. She dialed the number and it rang once.

"Hello?"

"Yeah, hello, it's Moira Barber. What I was say—"

"So, you want to know about the murders? Are you recording? What's the podcast called?"

Moira took a breath to calm herself. "Yes, I'm recording. The podcast doesn't have an official name; we're gathering the stories yet. What we're focusing on here is The Walking Son."

The man clicked his tongue. "Well now, haven't heard anybody drive that particular pig to market in a good long while. What do you know?"

"Uh, I'd rather hear what you know and then we can compare stories. That way I don't...you know, spoil the water, eh?"

"There's three theories about The Walking Son. The first is that he's a traveller caught in a time rift and he's stuck in some kind of loop that pulls him in and out of spots. Far as I know, this theory started when the police lost him, right from the cell they had him in. I know the official statement was that they let him go, but the theory says he just disappeared. I don't buy that one for a second.

"Next one deals with a ghost town we got, oh, twenty minutes south of Selma and about forty-five minutes from Blueville. Choohaba was a thriving town during the Civil War, an important town, too. See they had a big old military prison there called Castle Dexter, and story goes, The Walking Son was held captive there until the great flood in 1863, if I recall. Many Union soldiers broke free and The Walking Son was one of them and his only hope was to get back to his mother, but a Confederate soldier shot him when he was running down a road. So now his ghost is forever trying to get home to his mama. Another theory that doesn't sit quite like peach cobbler and vanilla ice cream. See, the police found coins in the man's pockets when they took him in. The money was old, but not that old. I've heard some say that money was new as 1945, so that kind of defeats that theory."

Moira nearly broke in that the coins were from 1876, all of them, but did not.

"The third theory, and this is the one I prescribe to, was that The Walking Son wasn't named Lewis like he said, he was named Thomas Daniel Lawless. He was thirty-one in 1965 and had escaped the overcrowded and underfunded Bryce Hospital, aka the Alabama State Hospital for the Insane. That picture was simply something he picked up somewhere along the way, the police did accidentally let him out—or he was just that crafty at escaping, as he'd escaped the asylum—and middle-aged men, dirty from the road and with scraggly beards sure do look alike when you put them side-by-side.

"There's a bit of interesting history around Bryce Hospital, that was over in Tuscaloosa, and it involves Governor George—"

"I heard something closer to the second one," Moira said, thinking simply about the coins. "Was the Civil War jail still active in eighteen-seventy-six?"

The old reporter and editor laughed. "Civil War was done and through in just under four years. I'll give you a pass on not knowing that 'cause you ain't from here."

"Oh, right. Of course. What happened to kill the town? Uh, Choohaba?" Moira said, pulling it from memory and then writing the town's name phonetically on the complimentary pad of paper next to the alarm clock and Bible.

"Few things, but mainly the flood in 'sixty-five just did too much damage. The town had a good deal of blood and the Freedmen were buying up the flood-wasted homes. The whites didn't want to stick around with all the coloreds. Eventually, the houses got to be so cheap that a colored fella bought up most of houses, took them apart, and carted them upriver to Selma.

"Choohaba has some interesting ghost tours in October if you're ever back this way. Come to think of it, coming from way up there to way down here is an awful piece of wandering for a story you're getting over the phone."

Moira was circling the name of the town on the notepad. "Wanted to get a feel for the place. Is there still much there, at Choohaba?"

"Some buildings, sure."

"This is so helpful. Do you mind if I call you back if I need clarification, Mr., uh…"

"James Lacey, and I don't mind at all. Don't get up to much, even less since that mess last year. It's got me paranoid as a frog on a hot plate. Given my age and weight class, and just how many years I enjoyed puffing on Marlboros, I think maybe it's the smart way to go about living, but I try not to let on to anybody I know I got a handful of reusable masks. They get touchy about that."

"Ah, ha, Mr. Lacey, thanks again."

Moira hung up before the old man had a chance to ramble further. Stephen was falling apart and she needed to keep him mobile.

"I think I know where we need to go, but we've got to figure out how to move you around."

Stephen's dry tongue played over his dry lips and he forced out two words: "Duct tape."

It was nearly the noon hour when Moira got Stephen wrapped with black duct tape and handed him the cheap crutches she'd purchased from a Rexall. He pushed to his feet and took a few tentative steps. He took a few more and turned around to go again. This would work, at least until his arms and hips failed.

The real bitch of it was the guessing and the mounting dread that came along with knowing the gradual changes were becoming less gradual and soon enough he might be a face on a newsstand. He might spend his last days unable to move. He might not make it until no pennies remained.

"Fuck," he whispered and reached for his wallet and the four coins.

Choohaba was easy enough to find and Moira had gone into the visitor's center, paid two bucks for a map, and then another thirty for the extended tour beginning in only fifteen minutes.

"I can't do a guided tour," Stephen said from the passenger seat of the truck.

"Oh, right," she said.

"I'll just rest. I'm exhausted."

Moira left him and Stephen turned in the seat and pulled the zipper on the luggage containing the bones. The scent was a little earthy, but not unpleasant. It reminded him of the bagged clay they used in high school art classes.

"We brought you home, what do you say you lift this..." he trailed, still having trouble saying the word, though was currently suffering its truths, "curse?"

He spied the bag, waiting for it to move, waiting for spiritual fingers to unzip it the rest of the way and relieve him of the burden. When nothing happened, he turned and faced the window. The sun had him sweating and he almost laughed when he thought *can't be good for my pages*, but the humor died, just as he would if Moira couldn't figure this out.

The hours mounted slowly and Stephen drank leftover beer and nibbled on cold fries hiding at the bottom of the KFC takeout bag. He spoke often to the bones and was in the middle of a series of questions when Moira opened the driver's side door. Her face was sunburnt and her eyes gleamed.

"There are two possibilities, I think. The place is a ghost town, and the employees think it's haunted, but none suggested there was any connection to The Walking Son myth, which sucks, but there is a cemetery and there is a list of names available on their website of everyone who lived here."

"Okay," Stephen said—he'd drank four beers and was feeling sorry for himself. "So I'm screwed?"

"What? No. Here's what we do. The place closes in ten minutes, I drop you and the bag—" She paused, seeing the zipper was open. "Did you open that?"

"Who else?"

Moira nodded. "Yeah, of course. Right. So, I drop you and the bag off on the way out, then I come back after dark with the shovel." Which was still in the back of the truck. "First, I look up which families lived here until around eighteen-seventy-six, find someone named Lewis on the list, and see what happens when we take the bones there. If that doesn't work, we bury them in the gravesite with everyone else who lived here."

Stephen began shaking his head in small, frantic turns. "That's so...fucking stupid! I'm fucking dead...because...that's the best...you could come up...with? Jesus fucking...Christ! How...in the–?"

Moira slapped him across the face. "Get a hold of yourself!"

Stephen rubbed his cheek.

"After tonight there's only three days and who knows what you'll look like tomorrow or Wednesday."

Stephen clenched his fists but let the anger drain. He looked out the window on the sparse green world that had once made up a town. "Fine. Drop me off and I'll wait."

"This could work, Stephen. Listen, it's possible. I've been thinking about what that hippie told us about the attack, when the man said, 'This time I'll get the help.' Don't you see, he's one of these unfinished business ghosts and didn't get help and now he's wandering," Moira said, growing a touch frantic herself. If she was right and all the leaps and coincidences played properly together, then she had it mastered. If it was correct, it was worth every ounce of passion she displayed because she was saving not just her husband, but her family.

"Yeah, okay," Stephen said. "Grab me something to drink when you come back, too."

Moira looked around the cab of the truck as if she'd forgotten that she'd left him there all afternoon. "Right, of course. I'll bring food, too."

At this, he shrugged. Still not hungry, but he had to keep his throat moisturized. It had begun to feel as if it would crack and eventually crumble if he didn't.

"We'll likely have to wait for dark to go in deeper, though. I saw cameras. Who knows if they have a security guard."

"Right," Stephen said, and scratched his cheek. A flake of skin dropped slowly like blown ash and he brushed it from his lap.

Sundown was slow coming. Moira had to wait until the moon was up and the security guard at the gate put in his headphones and closed his eyes. She'd parked a couple miles back the road and hoofed it, carrying a small bag of Gatorade bottles and snack foods—she'd grabbed a single burger from a roadside stand on her way back to town, knowing Stephen wouldn't want one. He was fading fast and she had to stay focused, and stay positive.

Stephen sat against a tree only fifty feet in from the gate. He had his cellphone out, and in the dark, the screen seemed like a homing beacon.

"Come on, the guard's just back there," she whispered and helped him stand.

They cut deeper into the small patch of forest and came out on the plot where the military prison had been. Not a twig of the building or fence remained, and only a plaque on a post gave away its former location. Willow trees had grown about the field, long white arms reaching for grass while simultaneously stretching forty feet into the sky.

"You want to sit?" Moira asked and when Stephen nodded, she helped him down, feeling the shift of his body beneath her grasp. It made her stomach churn. "When I was waiting for the guard to look somewhere else, after I walked up and down the road looking for another low spot in the fence, I checked the houses and who lived where. And guess what."

"Can I...get a drink?" Stephen said, his words harsh and dry.

"Oh, right. I brought food, too."

He accepted a Gatorade and it took much of what he had left to crack the seal. He downed a third and immediately vomited it up. Moira straightened and turned left and then right, listening for footfalls, watching for flashlight movement. Nothing. She leaned back in close and rubbed Stephen's shoulder. That loose edge book texture was right there beneath the shirt. Four coins notwithstanding, things were getting close.

"So, I found a place where the Bedford family lived, they had a son—who would've been twenty-nine in eighteen-sixty-seven. It didn't say if he still lived there, but he was part of the family."

"Okay." Stephen managed to down the remainder of the bottle, but dry swallowed like he had the spins, his breathing deep and his eyes glassy. "Moy," he said. It was a pet name from when they were dating, fallen away sometime after their wedding nearly twenty years prior.

"What?"

"I...love you. I don't think...I can move...no more."

"You have—"

Stephen shook his head and began crying quietly. "I'm not even...human. My arms are...all loose. I'm...drying. I just want...to go home."

Moira exhaled heavily through her nose and then sucked back tears. "Too bad," she said and looked around, seeking inspiration.

Trees and plaques on posts. Eyes closed, she tried to recall any information of value, as she'd read every one during the tour. There were a few foundations remaining. More than a mile away was a church. There were slaves' quarters a little further than that. A huge artisan well directed the ovular route of the town—keeping the residents close to water.

Bringing it in, across a road and through a patch of forest was the white cemetery. Miraculously, the front wall of a house stood where the rest of the home had disappeared. Not far from there was the Black cemetery. Several former foundations dotted the open spaces—all marked. One of those marked plots was where the Bedford family had lived until 1876.

Moira eyed Stephen, wondering just how in the hell...she rushed to the big luggage bag and set it on its side. She tossed out all the filler items—all the things she didn't mind losing—and lifted the rags and bones, gently, and set them in the grass. She pulled the open bag close to Stephen.

"Ready? You can help me or not, but this is how it has to happen," she said.

Stephen was pliable and pushed when necessary to get his ass over the seam where the bottom portion of the luggage mated with the top.

"This might hurt," Moira said, grabbing onto the ankle-shaped pages wrapped in duct tape. She bent the legs back to a tremendous chorus of crinkling paper. "Sorry." She grabbed the bottom zipper and reefed it up.

"Can't feel...below...my chest," Stephen said, so low, too low, his head and shoulder laid back out the other side of the luggage.

"Good, I guess. Now, I'm sorry about this, eh." Moira grabbed the bundle of bones and stuffed them in with Stephen. "Gotta zip the top some."

Stephen sighed when her firm but gentle grasp took hold of his head and face until she leaned his weight against her knee, helped Stephen move his arms into the bag, and zipped it far enough that only the top of his head down to his eyes poked out. He was so much less a person than he had been, and Moira choked on emotions.

"Ready?" she said and clicked the button for the telescoping handle. It popped and she tested the weight. It was slow going over the grass and onto the hard-packed gravel, but they were moving.

"I'm sorry...I helped...bury...you," Stephen mumbled.

Moira barely heard him over the quiet grind of plastic wheels on dirt, but she did hear him. She didn't like it. It was as if he'd given up already, as if he was trying to make peace when the damned war was still waging.

Along the road, the Bedford plot was more than two miles away and she had to slow and stop often enough that it would take more than two hours to get there. But she held it together and pulled.

As she moved, walking backward, mostly, she allowed herself to wonder about the next step. Up until then, fixing the situation was solved in increments and each followed something a little like rules. They discovered approximate location. Then they'd asked around. Then they'd asked for stories. Then she'd reached where to go. Now, the situation was going to fall into the hands of the supernatural acting out, and in their favor.

Or not.

Initially, it seemed as if the coins might simply incite a change. They were in Stephen's pants pocket and basically touching the man who'd owned them to begin with. That kind of contact had to stir up something—of course, she'd hoped general proximity would correct things, even thought it likely. If the coins wouldn't do it, taking the remains to a direct location or burial had to. To think otherwise was a waste of time. To think otherwise was to begin the grieving process.

"Are you okay?" Moira said, walking backward, one eye on the dark road and the other on the top of Stephen's bald head.

"Yeah," he said and sniffled.

Up until then, she'd never seen him cry. It wasn't who he was.

Add it to the list of things not to think about.

Cloud cover began to pass, lighting the way, which allowed Moira to read enough of the plaques along the road to know how close they were getting. A gentle breeze picked up as they rounded a corner. The river was louder there, helping dull the potential impact of the sound of the luggage wheels. Moira's shoulders loosened a hair, although her mind had been a million other places, part of her remained worried about that security guard in his booth, miles back.

The fifth lot along the recent section of road was the first target, but each lot was more than one hundred yards across and the foundation, in some cases, were another thirty deep into the lot.

The Bedford lot was not so deep and Moira left the luggage in the middle of the road for a moment, not believing her eyes in the dimness. But, even close up, the plaque read

BEDFORD and a trill played over her skin. This had to work.

"We're here."

Stephen grunted.

Moira grabbed the handle and pulled, momentarily teetering the shovel riding atop the bag. Though he'd lost weight, he was still heavy enough that moving in reverse with both hands on the grip was the only smooth way to travel, the only way over the grass. She pulled hard and fast. Sweat ran rivers down her arms and from her face. The ground beneath her stiffened and she straightened. Bricks and wood beams just beneath a layer of grass.

"I'm going to unzip and bring out the bones," she said and got to doing it.

Stephen lifted a hand from the luggage and his fingertips fluttered in the breeze. She tried to ignore it, lock the image away with all the emotions and thoughts that weren't proactive...but dammit, he was fading *so fucking fast!*

The bundle came out and she set it down in a space that would've been inside the home. Here they were sharp against the brown contours, expectant and needy. Minutes mounted and she dared not move.

Eventually, Stephen cleared his throat and said, "Let's try...the...graveyard."

Moira licked her teeth beneath her lips. One down, one to go. One down, the next *had* to work. She inhaled deeply and exhaled through her nose. It was so much hope put on chance and luck and unpredictable action.

She put the bones back into the luggage with Stephen and started away. The Black cemetery came upon them quickly after passing a wall of birch trees and the odd willow. The plaque was the biggest they'd passed since turning onto that road. There was a lot of history in a cemetery for former slaves in what was once a breeding ground for the

KKK and a meeting place of high-ranking Confederates.

Moira did not slow to consider any of the history. Ahead, through the long stretching shadows and the vast open spaces was the standing wall, which meant, directly across a road was the white cemetery. The speed picked up and her feet clapped against the soft dirt as she cut a corner, nearly losing the bag and the shovel. She looked over her shoulder often and the white stones rose like stalagmites.

"This is it," Moira said and yanked the luggage onto the grass.

She straightened up and for a moment, thought about the view from that home where the wall remained standing, and how off-putting that must've been to look out a window, onto a graveyard. The reverie was fleeting and she took up the shovel.

The grass was soft and a bit spongey that close to the river. She cut out a chunk of sod about three feet long and two wide. She set it aside and got to digging. This new grave would be front of the pack, next to the oldest of the markers. Down was slow and the tip of the shovel pinged and clanged against rocks and old cement. Moira grunted and growled, willing the dirt and obstructions away, an ear directed to the road, knowing they might get unlucky at any moment and have the guard decide to make his rounds.

Once the hole was two feet at its deepest spot, Moira ran to the luggage and unzipped the bottom portion. She said nothing to Stephen, time felt much, much shorter than it had even five hours ago. The bones clanked and whumped as they fell into the hole. Moira dropped to her knees and pulled the dirt over top of the bundle. She then grabbed the sod and draped it like a rug, fitting it as well as it would go, and then pounded it flat.

When she leaned back, her breath barrelled hot and wet from her lungs. She watched the grave and watched it some more. Seconds stretched into minutes and then into an hour.

"Moy," Stephen whispered. "Let's...go...home."

Moira's face screwed up ugly with emotion and finally the dam broke and the waterworks burst. It was all for naught and her family was ruined. Done. She flailed and flopped sideways, reaching and wrapping her arms, hugging the luggage, her head a foot below Stephen's. Tears streamed and Stephen cooed, though it hardly had the desired effect.

His voice sounded like tearing paper.

The moon was high and Moira got herself together to the point that she could zip the luggage enough and drag Stephen away, perhaps there was time to let him die at home, say goodbye to Paul.

"You should record a message for Paul," she said.

"Need...drink...first," he said.

"Yeah, in the truck." She wanted to say more, but the words refused her. "Ready?"

Stephen didn't answer and that didn't matter. She tipped the luggage and took two backward steps before stopping at a rustling sound in front of her. She lifted her head and watched the grass shift and bulge. The sod slid away and a skeletal arm reached free.

"Oh. My. God," she whispered.

The second arm whipped out and the dirt mound went airborne, as if launched via landmine. The skeleton had blue eyes and long hair and a long beard. Tendrils of humanity began rejoining the bone structure. A mouth formed first and Moira understood the expression, an angry sneer. A grey tongue slipped out and licked the lips as the beard began falling away, raining into the shadowy grass.

The skeleton pushed up to its chest and Moira wasn't about to stick around. She b-lined in reverse, eyes hard on the re-animating corpse as it fleshed out and rose to its feet. Still only partially there, it began running and Moira tried to match the intensity, but she was going backward and just wasn't quick enough.

"Dear God," she said and tried to spin, to run with the luggage behind her. The bag tipped and she stopped after a single dragged footstep to right it. The skeleton was more man and almost on top of them.

Moira yanked and reefed as she started away. Those blue eyes on her, seemed to burn through her. She stumbled over something–a brick driven into the ground–but managed to keep upright. Three more steps, the swishing thumps behind them, catching them. She stumbled again, and this time her eyes fell to the back of the sign they'd passed. She jumped and the luggage rolled flat as her back came into contact with something big and solid.

The skeleton had become a man. A young man in a white shirt and dark billowy slacks. He reached out long and skinny fingers, and Moira dove, draping her body over the luggage as if trying to contain the fallout of a grenade.

A gentle foot planted on her back and then a second, but both were gone, timed to match the erratic pace of her heartbeat. A click played a soft echo next to the rush of the river before hinges creaked open.

Moira couldn't help but look.

The remainder of the home formed around her. The main door had been pushed open, and glistening beneath the moonlight, someone had painted the word WITCH in blood upon the flaking, white-washed wood. Within, candelabras lined the walls and two men carried oil lamps and rifles. One of the men turned to the re-animated corpse and said, "We can't let Mama destroy this family. We can't let her burn through Papa's money surrounded by all them, now grow a heart, Lewis, and play the role of a strong brother."

The corpse, Lewis, nodded.

The other man nudged him in a way that meant to lend strength. "We can't let her do none of this. It ain't right and you know it, now sit tight."

The pair of men left Lewis behind and made for a door at the end of a hallway of fine but ruffled wallpaper and warbling wooden accents. They stepped through and one shouted, "We ain't lettin' you ruin this family, Mama! This place is a dead place and you buyin' up homes and doin' rites ain't gonna bring it back! Not when all them Freedmen stakin' claims! This place has become a black mark on the Confederation and all we stand for, Mama!"

The first shot rang out and then a second. Lewis' knees buckled and he leaned against a wall. A third shot rang out, and then a fourth.

No voices rose in explanation and the door did not open.

Lewis pushed up, but continued leaning, he started toward the door. Moira felt her body lifting and her limbs moving as if by the volition of an invisible stranger. She crawled after him and immediately smelled bread and wax and gunpowder and blood. Lewis was at the door but wasn't going through. Moira hurried to catch up.

"Mama?" he said.

"Lewis," a voice hissed back, feminine, but faded.

Lewis pushed through and Moira hurried in, sidling the swinging door. The room was a bloodbath. The two couches and the rocking chair lay askew. On the floor lay one Black woman, her face beneath the rising flames of a broken oil lamp, the two white adult brothers, one panting, wide-eyed but staring blankly, the other with a hole in his chest big enough to drop in a ping-pong ball, and an old white woman sprawled in a heavy dress, a hand to her chest and a rifle by her foot. Lewis ran toward the white woman.

"Put out the fire," she said.

Lewis changed direction and yanked a thick curtain down from a heavy brass-accented rod. He draped the dead woman and began patting the thick cotton where flames bit and licked. His foot kicked free a revolver that went spinning over the hardwood. Once the fire was out, Lewis slid on his knees to the white woman's side.

"Oh, Mama, I did not think they would do it! You must believe me! I am weak and they have always been willful!" He was sobbing around the screamed words.

"Listen to me, Son. You need to run and get help, worry about all this later. You get me help," the woman said, blood jumping out from the wound behind her fingers with every word.

Lewis popped to his feet, his entire upper-half nodding that yes he would, he'd been in the wrong, but would fix it. He tore out of the room. "I am so sorry, Mama!"

Moira watched him go, as did the woman. The woman then pawed around the floor and Moira rounded a small couch to get a better look. Ash lines had been drawn onto the floor: circles, a triangle, a pentagram. The woman had a book next to her and she was trying to read.

Moira understood then, this was her chance. "You need to lift the curse," she said. "You need to lift the curse!"

The woman's mouth started moving, her words an indistinguishable jumble.

Moira's hand passed through the woman, but she looked up and their gaze locked for two seconds. "It was a mistake, and my husband did not mean it. You have to lift the curse."

The woman fell back, a great whistle rang from the wound in her chest as she inhaled. She then shouted, "Protect my Lewis! Protect him for I have been your ser—" Her voice cracked and she gagged and coughed, spewing a great gout of blood before slumping forward.

Moira tried again to touch her, but her hand passed through, this time causing the woman to lessen, as if she'd been made of fog. The home drifted and rose. The bodies and furniture and every wall but one disappeared.

Without pause, Moira jerked upright and ran to Stephen—having to skirt the freestanding wall with the suddenly locked door along the way. She dropped to her knees and zipped the luggage open, spilling the paper man sideways. He turned and a small grin played upon his lips.

"I...love...you," he said.

It sounded as if someone had crumpled three balls of paper in quick succession.

"No. No!" Moira grabbed Stephen's hands, tiny cuts playing into her flesh. "No!" She leaned down and held him. Kissed his face.

"Hey! You there!" a voice said from far too close by.

A flashlight blazed and Moira sobbed into her husband's chest.

The security guard had felt bad enough to let them go—after he did a cursory check of the grounds in a golf cart—as long as they promised not to come back. Really, he appeared happy to be rid of them, as freakish as they looked: a man wrapped in duct tape and stashed in a suitcase and a filthy woman with teary eyes and bloody hands.

The sun peeked over the eastern horizon as Moira pulled off the highway and into a truck stop. She needed fuel for the first leg of the long trip homeward and Stephen needed liquids to moisten his throat. He had to record a video for his son and damned if he was going to be intelligible.

Hours burned away in solemn quiet. Moira listening to the radio and Stephen not all there. They passed Birmingham proper and kept on a little further down the highway. Moira drank two large coffees, one chasing the other, and had to pull into a rest stop to use the toilet.

Once she was gone, Stephen began practicing his words, finding if he sipped from the bottle after every sentence, the outcome could be understood with little strain. "Paul. Paul," he said. He coughed then and drank from a liter bottle of Evian, using both hands like a toddler because his fingers had gone to shit.

Moira returned quickly, swung open the door and slammed it shut after her, jingling the three old pennies on the dash. Her cheeks were tear-streaky again and it broke Stephen's heart anew. He'd slept most of the time spent with the security guard and over the hour and a half between the truck stop and the rest stop. He'd have to nap again soon.

"Should we do the video, while you're…?" Moira let the silence say more than words could.

"Next stop. I want…to think…about…what I'll…say."

Moira took a deep breath through her nose and turned the key. She backed out and onto the merge lane. Traffic on the highway was sparse, perhaps because of the fogbank settling in over the last half-hour. The temperature was cooler than the days preceding, which was a minor blessing, but didn't let Moira open it up much when it came to the gas pedal.

"You know, whatever you say will have to do," Moira said and reached over to fiddle with the radio tuner. "Paul needs something, if he can't have his father." The radio was all static and refusing to scan past emptiness, instead of falling on scratchy stations, as if to force an audience. "Damn thing."

"Stop. Stop," Stephen said, his eyes wide and pinned to the side of the road. "Stop!"

Moira finally looked at him, easing off the gas and pulling to the sun-paled shoulder. She hit the brakes gently and a cloud of asphalt dust plumed in their wake. "What? What is it?" she said.

Stephen turned in his seat, difficult as that was.

"What?" Moira said again, also watching out the back window.

Through the fog and dust, a young man jogged up behind them. He had nothing in his hands and only his clothes with him. He was grinning through the first notes of a beard shadow.

Stephen fumbled for the button on his window. The glass came down just as the young man came around.

"So glad you stopped, felt like I been walking forever," he said.

Stephen coughed. "Where. Where...you headed?"

It was him, Lewis. The Walking Son. He was back and he was on the move.

"Far as I can get."

Stephen worked at his door and got it open. "Push me...forward...and climb...in," he said.

"Thank ya, kindly. Y'all from the north?"

Moira's jaw trembled as understanding finally set in a way she could reconcile, a way that fought against the future she'd only just begun to allow herself to believe. "Canada," she said.

"Holy, you going that far?" Lewis smiled and straightened himself. "Can't remember if I ever been to Canada. Ain't that the damndest thing?"

Stephen nodded and pointed to the items on the dashboard. "Are you...thirsty? Hungry?"

"Oh, geez, sure could go for a candy bar and since you're offer—hey, those pennies? I just about love different coins."

Moira pulled back out onto the highway, the fog suddenly gone and the temperature rising, pouring in through Stephen's open window. "Do you want them back?" she asked.

"Back?" Lewis said, cocking his head a touch sideways.

"Back...there," Stephen said. "Do you...want them...back...there?"

"Oh, right. Sure, and the candy bar, since you're offering."

Stephen tried to grab the coins, but couldn't and Moira swatted his hand away, taking a new cut along the knuckle of her thumb. She held the coins out and into the back seat, glancing only briefly at the grinning young man.

"Drop'em and I'll catch'em," Lewis said.

She did and they clanged into his palms. Stephen reached for the Snickers bar Lewis had been eyeing, it was big enough and light enough that he could pick it up, and spun to hand it off.

"Jesus," Stephen whispered. "Look."

Moira turned to see. There was nobody there.

It happened slowly, little by little, through Alabama, Mississippi, Arkansas, Missouri, Iowa, South Dakota, Wyoming, Washington, and finally into British Columbia, the pages of Stephen Barber's body solidified, and the words came away in scabs. His voice returned, as did his appetite. He never shot the film for his son and Moira let herself relax.

"Guess I ought to stop by the police station." Stephen rubbed his smooth head as they pulled into town.

"What will you tell them?"

"Only as much as they'd believe," Stephen said.

"So, nothing?"

Stephen grinned. He might tell them a little more than that; then again, he might be a due for a break from stories.

ABOUT THE AUTHOR

Eddie Generous has fallen off three different roofs and been lit on fire on multiple occasions. He grew up on a farm and later slept with his shoes under his pillows in homeless shelters. He dropped out of high school to afford rent on a room at a crummy boarding house, but eventually graduated from a mediocre college. He is the author of several small press books, has 2.8 rescue cats (one needed a leg amputation), is a podcast host, and lives on the Pacific Coast of Canada.

You can find Eddie online at www.jiffypopandhorror.com

The Seventh Terrace

Visit us online at
www.the-seventh-terrace.com

ALSO AVAILABLE FROM THE SEVENTH TERRACE

Unfortunate Elements of My Anatomy

Terrace VI – Forbidden Fruit

Terrace VII – Wall of Fire

Trace & Solomon: Torrington

Sleeping Underwater

The Black City Beneath

End of the Loop

Futility: Orange Planet Horror

Infractus

Fishing with the Devil

Unfortunate Elements of My Anatomy
By **Hailey Piper**

Love twisted into horrific shapes, nightmares driven by cruel music, and a world where what little light remains fractures the sky into midnight rainbows in eighteen stories tracing the dark veins of queer horror, isolation, and the monstrous feminine.

The universe unwinds to the tune of a malicious ice cream truck jingle in "We All Scream". "The Law of Conservation of Death" dictates that a ghost pursue his prey across her every reincarnation. Superstitions thrive even in the distant future and across the stars when a colony shuttle mounts a witch trial in "Hairy Jack". And try to "Forgive the Adoring Beast" as it scavenges a world of dead gods for tokens of bloody affection.

Including two new short stories and a never-before-published novelette, *Unfortunate Elements of My Anatomy* digs deep inside and clings to the beating nightmare heart you always knew was there.

Starseed
By **Stephen Guy**

In a world illuminated by gaslight, a wealthy, debauched dandy's mentor tests the limits of conscience with a series of human-alien hybridization experiments, facilitated by the decryption of a forbidden text now known as the Voynich Manuscript.

Not knowing what it is they've unleashed, mayhem ensues, with hired killers, Brazilian Wandering Spiders, and shady professionals willing to undertake the performance of any act that one should be ashamed to ask for. There is flesh, and the power that holds. Juices run, blood flows, and ichor oozes. The dandy soon comes to learn that wealth cannot buy love, the past exists for nothing so much as to haunt the present, and as long as there is desire, the Star Flower will procure what it needs to bloom, and spread its seed through the cosmos.

Terrace VI: Forbidden Fruit
Curated by **Sarah L. Johnson and Robert Bose**

Welcome to the Sixth Terrace of Dante's tower of Purgatory, serving up sins of gluttony in an eternal banquet. On this carefully curated menu you'll find children stuffing themselves to death, a forgotten saviour gorging on

cheeseburgers between bareknuckle rounds on the roadhouse circuit, wealthy socialites revel in an orgiastic alien feast, and the end of days as seen through an apocalyptic carnival of indulgence. Excessive consumption also manifests in darker hungers, for cruelty, for distraction, or possession. A pair of grifters bent on having it all chase a Scottish leprechaun across the English countryside, a newly deceased addict vies for the attention of Heavenly Higher Ups, degenerate poker players gamble with unforeseen currency, and when an old lady swallows a fly, it's just the beginning.

Featuring stories and art by Mike Thorn, Robin van Eck, Eddie Generous, Cam Hayden, Julie Hiner, Konn Lavery, Sarah L. Johnson and Robert Bose.

www.ingramcontent.com/pod-product-compliance
Lightning Source LLC
Chambersburg PA
CBHW060603190726
48283CB00003B/1133